## "Careful, Nicolas, or you'll make me break a promise to myself."

"What promise?"

Her gaze bored into his. "To keep my hands and lips off you."

"How can I convince you to break that promise over and over again?" He'd never met anyone quite like Chloe—pretty, genuine, unique...and he'd already seen how flexible she was. His imagination heated up.

"Nicolas..."

"Yes, sexy?"

She bit her lip. "Sorry. I never expected to hear my teenage dream call me that. It's a little overwhelming."

"Sexy? I'm just a man. And you are a very desirable woman. Two people who can make one another very happy."

"It's not that simple. I'm on the job and you are..." She let out a breath. "You are my Nicky M."

He smiled. He liked that, the way she had possessed him. "I can be yours tonight in the flesh. Let me make all your dreams come true. Say yes."

\* \* \*

*Star-Crossed Scandal* is part of
the Plunder Cove trilogy.

Dear Reader,

When I was eighteen, I traveled to South America to meet up with a friend. Flying to a foreign country by myself where I had a limited grasp of the language was terrifying. Plus, the plane had technical problems and was stuck on the tarmac for two hours! Being a melodramatic teenager, I was sure I was going to die. I started to cry and a young Brazilian guy got up from his seat and asked to join me. He was cute, sweet and very kind. He gave me his phone number to call him when I got to Rio at the tail end of my trip. He and his gracious family welcomed me into their home. Chris, his sister, became my Brazilian sister. I credit her for helping with the Portuguese words and context to sketch out Nicolas Medeiros.

Nicolas was an international teenage heartthrob. But he was more than that to Chloe Harper. His music, videos and poster helped her survive her tough childhood. Now that she is a grown woman with stardom of her own, she is tasked to work with sexy Nicolas to help her family's resort.

Thank you for reading!

*Kimberley Troutte*

# KIMBERLEY TROUTTE

———

## STAR-CROSSED SCANDAL

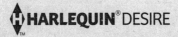

HARLEQUIN® DESIRE

Recycling programs
for this product may
not exist in your area.

ISBN-13: 978-1-335-60372-2

Star-Crossed Scandal

Copyright © 2019 by Kimberley Troutte

This is a work of fiction. Names, characters, places and incidents are either the product of the author's imagination or are used fictitiously, and any resemblance to actual persons, living or dead, business establishments, events or locales is entirely coincidental.

This edition published by arrangement with Harlequin Books S.A.

For questions and comments about the quality of this book, please contact us at CustomerService@Harlequin.com.

® and TM are trademarks of Harlequin Enterprises Limited or its corporate affiliates. Trademarks indicated with ® are registered in the United States Patent and Trademark Office, the Canadian Intellectual Property Office and in other countries.

Printed in U.S.A.

**Kimberley Troutte** is a RITA® Award–nominated, *New York Times*, *USA TODAY* and Amazon top 100 bestselling author. She lives in Southern California with her husband, two sons, a wild cat, an old snake, a beautiful red iguana and various creatures Hubby and the boys rescue.

To learn more about her books and sign up for her newsletter, go to kimberleytroutte.com.

### Books by Kimberley Troutte

**Harlequin Desire**

*Plunder Cove*

*Forbidden Lovers*
*A Convenient Scandal*

Visit her Author Profile page at Harlequin.com, or kimberleytroutte.com, for more titles.

You can find Kimberley Troutte on Facebook, along with other Harlequin Desire authors, at Facebook.com/harlequindesireauthors!

Dedicated to anyone who has
felt mistreated or invisible.

Know that you are not alone and love
is our greatest strength of all.

# History of Plunder Cove

For centuries, the Harpers have masterminded shrewd business deals.

In the 1830s, cattle baron Jonas Harper purchased the land grant of Plunder Cove on the now affluent California coast. It's been said that the king of Spain dumped the rich land because pirates ruthlessly raided the cove. It is also said that no one saw a pirate ship after Jonas bought the land for a rock-bottom price paid with pieces of eight.

Harpers pass this tale on to each generation to remind their heirs that there is a pirate in each of them. Every generation is expected to increase the Harper legacy, usually through great sacrifice, as with oil tycoon RW Harper, who sent his children away ten years ago.

Now RW has asked his children to return to Plunder Cove—with conditions. He is not above bribery to get what he wants.

Harpers don't love; they pillage.

But if RW's wily plans succeed, all four Harpers, including RW, might finally find love in Plunder Cove.

# One

Hot, dreamy sex.

That's what the man stepping out of the limo exuded. And pulsing music. If Nicolas Medeiros was a song, he'd be a Brazilian beat, throbbing with dance, liquid fire and lyrics a girl couldn't get out of her head.

Standing between her two brothers at the entrance to the Plunder Cove resort, Chloe Harper had a moment to drink Nicolas in while he talked on his cell phone and waited for the driver to bring his luggage out of the trunk. The long sleeves of his sharkskin-gray shirt were rolled up to reveal tanned, muscular forearms. His dark charcoal slacks accentuated his thin waist, and his suit jacket was casually slung over one shoulder. He was the adult version of the teen heartthrob Chloe Harper had fallen in love with a long time ago.

She fanned herself.

"Are you okay?" Jeff, her brother closest to her in age, wrapped his arm around her shoulder. "You look like you're about to pass out."

"Hell, you, too?" Matt, her oldest brother, grumbled as he studied her. "This morning Julia had that same look on her face when I mentioned that Nicolas Medeiros was coming to town and staying at the resort. What's the big deal?"

"He's a big deal," Chloe whispered.

Nicky M had been a pop star legend back in the day, and now he was a huge music producer who had discovered several of the biggest names on the charts. He was a legend! More than that, he was…her Nicky M. When she was eleven years old, Chloe had kissed his poster every night before she went to sleep. He'd been her savior when no one else cared. And now her crush was striding up the walk of her family's resort with those dancing hips. And if they made a good enough impression, he'd sign a deal to do his next pop music reality show here.

As the resort's activities director, she was the one who would be showing him around. Her family had given her the task of getting his name on the dotted line.

They'd be spending a lot of time together.

She made a strange noise at the back of her throat that sounded like a closed-off squeal.

"Oh, man. You've got it bad. Maybe we should give the job to someone else," Matt teased.

"Don't you dare!" she said way too loudly. Nicky

M—correct that, *Mr. Medeiros*, her *guest*, her *job*, looked up from his call.

"Relax, Chloe," Jeff said out of the corner of his mouth. "Dad wants the deal to work and so do I. Medeiros and his music production company are the next step in building the resort to its full glory. It's up to you to convince him that he needs us."

She shot Jeff a dirty look. "Is that supposed to make me relax?"

Matt laughed. "Just do your thing, sis. He's a guy. He'll love you."

She bit her lip. Oh, she'd spent many lonely nights fantasizing about being loved by Nicky M, all right, but that's not what her brother meant.

"Mr. Medeiros!" Jeff offered his hand. "Welcome to Casa Larga Resort at Plunder Cove. I'm Jeffrey Harper, the executive director of the resort and restaurant."

Nicolas put his cell phone away and the two men shook hands.

"You remember Matt, your pilot from LA," Jeff said. While Jeff ran the operations of the family's resort empire, Matt pursued his passion of flying. He offered flights to important resort guests and volunteered his skills with locals in need.

"Of course. The flight was short and sweet. You are a very good pilot." Nicolas shook hands with Matt, too.

Oh…that voice! His deep, melodious Brazilian Portuguese accent had played a part in quite a few of Chloe's fantasies. She wished he'd take off those dark sunglasses. She longed to see his eyes.

*Stop it!* She warned herself. She shouldn't be longing to see any of his body parts. Chloe had made a deal with herself to steer clear of men for a while and was determined to keep it. Looking was fine, but acting on her desires was out of the question.

"Dad sends his apologies for not meeting you himself. He's not feeling well," Jeff said poignantly.

That was an understatement. The last time Chloe had checked in on her father, he'd been sitting in his room with the shades drawn, fighting the downward spiral into his dark place. Her father had fought with untreated depression for decades. She'd dealt with the dangerous effects of it as a small child, before the stress led to her parents' divorce, but then she'd left the family estate with her mother. And she hadn't understood her dad's mental illness until she saw it up close. If he didn't come out of it soon, Chloe would disobey his wishes and bring a psychiatrist into the home, the rumor mill be damned. RW Harper was a powerful man and few people bucked his orders, but she was worried about him and would do whatever it took to help him.

"That is too bad. I was hoping to talk to the great RW Harper. Plus, I have questions about the contract he sent me," Nicolas said.

"He'll make time for that during your stay," Jeff said smoothly. "This is Chloe, the resort's activities director. She'll take care of all of your needs for the week."

Jeff meant *business* needs. So why did her gaze take a sudden roam across Nicolas's body. Broad shoulders, narrow waist... She forced her eyes back up to his face. He was watching her.

Her cheeks were on fire. A trickle of sweat ran down her back.

She stretched her hand out and was beyond relieved it wasn't shaking. "Welcome to Casa Larga."

"Chloe. I like that name." He lifted his dark glasses, and his gray-blue eyes locked on to hers and melted her insides. She was seriously going to pass out if she didn't figure out how to breathe around the man.

He held her hand for several long beats. A Brazilian custom or her own hand refusing to let go? Chloe removed her hand but couldn't unlock her gaze from his. She used to wonder what had happened to a boy to make his gray eyes project such a soulful expression. The man before her still had the look, but now it was mixed with mature comprehension, as if he knew exactly what she was thinking. His eyebrow lifted as if he could see the desperate desire pulsing inside her.

Oh, God, did he know what she was thinking?

Because she suddenly wanted to break all her rules for him.

Matt chuckled beside her. "Hell, guess some things are a bigger deal than I thought. I'd better go give my wife some lovin'. See you all later." Heading toward his motorcycle, he gave Chloe a thumbs-up.

Surely Matt didn't think their guest was attracted to her. Nicolas Medeiros dated supermodels and pop stars. Although she was an heiress to the great Harper fortune and a celebrity yoga teacher in her own right, she was no supermodel. She rarely wore makeup and believed in enhancing the inner natural beauty of a person through spiritual awakening. Nicolas, on the other hand, dated women who had professional makeup artists on staff.

"Right this way, Mr. Medeiros." Jeff motioned for Nicolas to step into the entryway.

Nicolas held back and gave her a look that heated her skin. "Ladies first."

Walking ahead of him, she wondered where his gaze was—on the low dip in her blouse, exposing her back, on her butt, or on the ten-foot crystal chandelier overhead?

Jeff guided their guest to the foyer, where building plans were spread out across the marble table. "The restaurant will officially open to the public at the end of the week. However, the staff is eager to serve you now. They need the practice."

"Complimentary, of course," Chloe said softly and then stepped back to let Jeff do his thing.

Nicolas's cell phone buzzed. He checked the text and shook his head before returning his attention back to them. "Sorry. Work."

She hoped to help him unplug from work during his stay. Nicolas was a big music producer, but everyone deserved a little downtime. It was her personal mission as an activities director and yoga teacher to help people learn how to live in the moment. To relax.

"Would you mind telling us about your show? It'll help me gauge what sorts of activities to prepare for the contestants," Chloe said.

"*If* we choose the Harper's resort for the show," Nicolas said. "There are three properties under consideration."

"Oh, I understand." She looked him in the eye. "I intend to help you make your decision. And choose us, of course."

"Intriguing." His lips quirked and she couldn't help but wonder what it would be like to kiss those lips for real.

"*Song of the Heart* is a reality show." His voice gave her a tiny shiver up her back. "Ten singer-songwriter contestants live together in a luxury setting, write songs and compete for a million-dollar music contract."

"I love it," she said.

"I'm very familiar with reality shows. We can help yours be a success," Jeff said as a nod to his past career as the host of *Secrets and Sheets*, a hidden camera critique of luxury hotels. "Let's look at the resort blueprints and see where the contestants would spend their time and where you could set up the camera crews. The resort will be ready for guests in eight months, but if your show needs it earlier, Harper Industries will make it work..."

As Jeff talked, Nicolas studied the plans while Chloe studied him.

He had a cropped beard and his hair was dark, thick and cut short. His shoulders were broad. Her schoolgirl crush had matured, but his gaze still had the power to turn her insides to mush.

Nicky M had always been more than a poster boy to her. She'd fancied herself a singer-songwriter once and had truly appreciated Nicky M's talent. He'd drawn a young, scared girl out of *her* dark place and lit up her imagination. He'd lifted her heart with his lovely words and beautiful melodies. She owed him more than he'd ever know.

But she didn't have any business fantasizing about Nicolas now. She wasn't hooking up with anyone until she got her own life under control. She had to learn how to love herself before she could love anyone else. Until that happened? She wasn't sleeping with any man. Not even super sexy Nicky M. She had a job to do.

Her father had tasked her with showing their guest all that Plunder Cove had to offer so that he'd agree to film his show at the new resort. Her dad's exact words were, "Don't let the man leave without signing the contract, Chloe. I'm counting on you."

She'd been desperate to please her father her entire life and had failed at every turn. A small part of her still wondered if that was why he'd banished her from Plunder Cove years ago, sending her to live with her mother after the divorce—because she wasn't good enough to be a Harper.

In the past, her parents had crushed her spirit. They'd broken her family, sent her away and taken away the music she'd loved. But she'd found her own path through yoga, and she was doing everything she could to heal herself. She'd even returned home not too long ago and reestablished a relationship with her older brothers. She was determined to prove she was worthy of her family's famous name.

She wouldn't fail at this.

How hard could it be to keep her hands and lips to herself and get a man to sign a few pieces of paper?

Even if he was the sexiest man on the planet.

* * *

Nicolas stopped listening to Jeff Harper's spiel about the building plans the moment he noticed the *gostosa* eyeing him.

The gorgeous activities director had a stunning figure. A brown skirt molded to her hips like dark chocolate on a strawberry. Her red crepe blouse dipped low in the back and was not quite see-through but made him want to strain his vision. The long blond braid intrigued him, but it was her aquamarine eyes that really got to him. When they locked on to his, he saw golden feathers within the blue irises. Amazing and deeply magnetic.

Strange. He wasn't usually so poetic. Not anymore. "The resort will be ready in time for your show." Jeff's voice drew Nicolas's gaze away from Chloe. "We guarantee it."

*Of course he'd say that.* The man was a Harper. RW Harper, Jeff's father, had the reputation for being a scheming, sneaky bastard. But also a savvy one. This hotel empire would be the most luxurious one in the nation, maybe the world. That was why Nicolas was here. He was after a contract for a big beautiful property to showcase his show. Funny, in the past he would have been looking for a quiet, beautiful spot on the beach to sit and write music. He wouldn't be on the phone or in meetings making deals, no, he would have been making music. Those days were over. He'd moved from making his own songs to making stars.

"That's about it. I'd better get back to the site. I'll leave you in Chloe's capable hands." Jeff walked out the door, leaving Nicolas alone with the beauty.

She stepped closer, moving with the poise and grace of a dancer. He was fully aware of her soft curves and was intrigued by the toned muscles in her arms and back. She had an athlete's body.

"I'll show you to your room," she said.

Nicolas enjoyed the sound of her voice. It had a rich, pure tone, with a slight emotional crack in it—fragility mixed with strength. *Leather and lace.*

"As the man said." Nicolas grinned. "I am in your hands."

"I'll do my best to handle your, uh…" A pretty pink blush traveled up her neck. She cleared her throat. "…needs."

He looked forward to seeing what her best was.

She led him down the hallway, her stride matching his. "I like the concept of your show, Nicky—excuse me—*Mr. Medeiros.*"

"Nicolas. I do, too. I support singer-songwriters and am looking for talent that is different, unique."

"Brilliant," she sighed. "Helping young artists is exactly what I thought you'd do when you got old." She covered her mouth. Her pretty eyes were wide. "I mean, you're not old now, just, you know, mature. Handsome."

"Thanks." She was a tongue-tied and adorable fan. He was used to woman falling over themselves around him, but he wanted Chloe to relax and treat him like a regular guy. He smiled. "People gave me a hand when I got started. I work hard to give back to the industry."

They passed a grand hall. Soft music played in the background. When they walked under one of the largest chandeliers he'd ever seen, the fractured light cast dancing stars across the tiled floors. Enchanting, yet hard to compare to the brilliance in Chloe's blue eyes. She led the way up a winding stairway, her beaded sandals snapping with each step. He noticed her toenail polish. Purple. His favorite color. His gaze traveled from those beautiful feet up to her toned legs.

*Santa Mãe*, she had a great figure. He wouldn't mind spending time with this beauty, nothing serious, of course, just short-term, hot sex.

"You've such a lyrical gift for storytelling. Those contestants are lucky to have an amazing songwriter like you to mentor them," she said.

He *used* to have the gift, but the muse had left him without any good stories to tell. Now he made money, not poetry. He was okay with that, and if he sometimes missed songwriting, he just reminded himself of how far he'd come. His success was worth the price of any small dissatisfactions. He would never go hungry again. But why tell her all that?

Instead he said, "Thank you."

Did she know how he'd been discovered? Most of the tabloids had reported some version of the truth. None knew all the nightmarish details about why he'd spent every moment from age ten to this day supporting his mother and four sisters. Singing was the only thing he had been able to do to repay his bottomless debt. Every penny he'd made went to his family. Until he'd had more than any of them would ever need.

And yet somehow it never felt like enough.

Still his *mãe* loved it when he sang and he loved to make her smile. "Your songs are made of stardust,

Nicky," his mother had said as her tiny cracked fingers hand-washed clothes for other families. "A blessing from the saints!"

An American music manager had seen him perform for tourists on Ipanema Beach and promised to make him a star. He'd been sixteen then, full of drive and blind trust. He'd allowed the manager to record him, and the first song hit all the charts. Nicky M was a sudden sensation. He flew to California on the back of that one song, trusting that riches were right around the corner. He'd planned to buy his family a home and get them out of the slums. *Mãe* wouldn't have to work so hard and his sisters could focus on school.

It was a poor-boy success story. The tabloids loved it.

But they hadn't printed the whole truth. How could they? Some secrets were too shameful to tell.

The manager he'd trusted siphoned money from Nicolas's bank accounts until there had been nothing left. Only months after leaving home, he'd been sixteen, scared and alone in a country where he barely spoke the language. There was no money to send home. He didn't have enough funds for an airline ticket. His mother and young sisters had been forced to find extra jobs cleaning rich people's homes to survive. They all went hungry.

The experience had hardened him.

It was the first of many painful disappointments. The industry battered him and taught him the most important lessons of his life: people lie, steal and use one another to get what they want.

It had taken cunning, luck and persistence to move from a pop star to the music producer who called the shots.

Nicolas trusted no one but himself. He worked his ass off to stay at the top. In those early years, lyrics had swelled up from deep within him, and music pulsed through his bloodstream. He had the natural ability to create eternal truths that people loved to listen to. He didn't have to work at writing music. It just happened, like breathing. The press had called him "the greatest Latin songwriter of our time."

But songwriting had become music production, the business, and star-making. He'd exchanged lyrics for the constant buzz of his phone, the high of making millions on others' stories.

And then…the music stopped.

The stardust had blown away, and the silence was like a death. He didn't have time to grieve the loss. Instead he spent every waking moment looking for the next star. He'd found fame, money, women—a lifestyle most people could only imagine.

There was no joy in it. But he told himself joy didn't make millions.

"Mr. Medeiros, we're going to be together a lot this week…" He wanted to imagine the breathiness in her voice wasn't solely from walking up the stairs. "I feel, um, I should tell you something."

He leaned closer. "Chloe has a secret?"

Her blue eyes shimmered. "I had a tiny crush on you when I was a girl."

Every now and then his past came in handy, especially when a beautiful woman seemed to appreciate his talent. Or, at least, the talent he used to have. Maybe this sexy blonde with the long braid and "kiss me" lips still remembered who he used to be.

They were on the landing on the top floor.

He pressed his hand to his heart, pretending to be wounded. "Only tiny? Not a man-size crush?"

"Honestly, it was more than tiny." She chuckled. He loved the richness of the sound. "I named my iguana after you. Little Nicky M."

He cocked his eyebrow. "Was he a handsome lizard?"

"Very. A red iguana with pretty eyes. Almost as amazing as yours."

Perhaps she would be his beautiful distraction for a few days. He needed a break and sleeping with a sexy fan would help him feel like himself, not the high-powered producer, for a while.

"We are going to get along fine, Chloe. Remind me to thank RW." It was a stroke of genius to send Chloe his way. But if Harper thought a sexy woman would drive Nicolas wild enough to instantly sign a contract, the man was wrong.

Nicolas could be as ruthless as RW when it came to the music business.

"Oh, no. My father can't know!"

*Father?* "You are a Harper, too?"

"Yes. I thought you knew. Didn't I say so? Sorry. I got a little excited when we met." She bit her lip. "Way too excited. Even now I'm having trouble—" she fanned herself "—getting my words out. Which is exactly why my father might not want me to work with you. If he knew about my huge…" Her gaze dipped toward Nicolas's crotch and bounced back up to his eyes again. Her cheeks flushed. "Uh, infatuation. When I was *younger*."

He spoke, his words low. "It will be our secret, then."

"I'll be completely professional with you—I promise." She crossed her heart, which had the effect of drawing his gaze to her chest.

"*Que pena.* Are you sure there's not any infatuation left?" Stepping closer, he looked into her eyes and pinched the air with his thumb and forefinger. "A flicker?"

Her breath hitched. She tried to play it straight, but her full lips seemed to want to turn up of their own accord. He liked the dimples in her cheeks. They reminded him of sideways smiles, and he had the urge to caress one of them with the back of his hand.

She blinked, clearly flustered. "A flicker, sure, but I want you to trust that I'll be…"

"Professional?" he finished for her.

"Yes." Her voice cracked. The way her gaze locked on to his told him she was into him, even if she didn't want to admit it.

He noticed they'd stopped in front of a door. "Is this my room?"

"Yes." She took a key ring out of her pocket, unlocked a door and held it for him to step inside. "Mine is just down the hall. Let me know if there is anything you need."

When he passed her, he inhaled the coconut scent of her shampoo. Did she taste as good as she smelled?

She licked her bottom lip as if she'd heard his thoughts.

The suite had a large sitting room, wet bar, over-stuffed leather couch, full-size desk and large patio.

"There is something I need," he said circling back to her.

He could hear her swallow. "Name it."

Leaning against the door frame, he crossed his arms. "A date for dinner tonight. Will you be mine?"

Her breath came out in a rush. "Me?"

He was thoroughly intrigued by the blush traveling up her neck. What was she thinking? Whatever it was, he liked it. He usually avoided starstruck fans, but she was too tempting for his usual caution.

"Yes, *gata*, you."

She blinked. "Did you call me a cat?" Her voice was barely a whisper.

"*Gata* is a term of endearment in Brazil. *Gatinha*, as well, which means kitty. Would you prefer I say *sexy*?"

"*Gata,*" she tried the word on for size. "I like it."

Her gaze dropped to his mouth. Pure heat flashed between them.

He wanted to kiss her. Tasting a stranger was noth-ing new for him. Women still threw themselves at him. Wild hookups came with the territory as a musician. As a producer, he still had his pick of women, though he was careful not to mix business with pleasure. He en-joyed sex. But as he'd gotten older, he started to think he was missing something—a real life with deep, lov-ing relationships.

But he wasn't the picket fence, loving wife and two kids in the yard kind of a guy. He'd left Hollywood for Plunder Cove because of the show and because he had a rather public breakup with a supermodel. It was better for him to stick with short-and-sweet-while-it-lasted flings. A pretty blonde fan might be exactly what he needed right now.

"Seven o'clock?" he pressed.

Her lips parted but no words came out. Some emotion he couldn't read passed over her face. Worry? Sadness?

*Droga.* Was she going to decline?

"Say yes, Chloe."

"Nicolas, there's something I should tell you…" she began in a tone that did not bode well for him.

His phone rang. *"Merda,"* he cursed. "Sorry. Give me a moment to take this."

To his disappointment, Chloe used the phone distraction as her chance to walk away from him. For some reason, that hurt.

Just before his door closed, she said the word he desperately needed to hear.

"Yes."

# Two

Contrary to what he'd led his daughter to believe, RW was not going to stay curled up in a dark room all day.

His chest hurt and the pain behind his eyeballs was excruciating, but he wasn't staying in bed. Not today. He waited until Chloe went down to greet their guest before sneaking out the back to take care of business.

His daughter had a job to do and so did he.

Even if his children didn't know it.

Shielding his eyes from the California sunshine, he strode across the patio and took a seat across from the first woman he'd ever loved—Claire Harper. It had been ten years since she'd walked out on him, taking their daughter with her. She'd arrived back in Plunder Cove for Jeffrey's wedding two months ago, and for some damned reason she was still here. He'd invited her for a late lunch today to get to the bottom of what she wanted.

"Claire, you do not age," he said.

She smiled at the compliment, but the fine lines around her eyes and lips hardly creased. Her forehead was smoother than he remembered. Ah, so that's where some of the millions he'd sent her had gone.

A flash of Angel, the woman he loved now, entered his mind. He preferred a real lady who came with wrinkles and flaws. A woman who could accept his flaws, as well.

Dealing with Claire was the first step in bringing Angel back to him.

"And you seem—" she studied him "—healthy."

He wasn't. Not yet. Still, he was much better than he'd been when he had lived with Claire.

"I'm impressed with this place. Our son did all this?" Claire motioned to the restaurant.

Where they sat under the eaves, it was easy to see that the amazing wood-and-glass structure resembled a pirate ship. It was an architectural masterpiece that was sure to grace the pages of magazines for years to come.

"That boy has come alive with this resort and restaurant project. I'm so proud of him."

A waiter arrived carrying one plate of pasta that he sat down in front of Claire.

"I went ahead and ordered my lunch. Wasn't sure you'd show," Claire said.

"I'm here, Claire. This is my home."

The waiter nervously stood by him. "Sorry to interrupt. Would you like anything, Mr. Harper?"

"Just a glass of water. Thanks."

The waiter quickly walked away.

"Water? Not bourbon and Wagyu steak?" Claire wound the fettuccine carbonara around her spoon and took a bite. As she chewed, her face tried to screw up into her old expression of disgust, but her forehead refused to budge. "The sauce is horrid."

"Impossible. Our chef is acknowledged as a top chef on both coasts."

Tentatively, she licked the sauce on her spoon. "It's spoiled!" She scrubbed her cloth napkin over her tongue.

A satisfied smile crept over his lips, for he knew what Michele had done. God, he loved his daughter-in-law. "I wouldn't eat the rest of that."

Claire swigged her pinot to cleanse her palate only to find a tiny bandage at the bottom of the glass. The look of horror on her face made his entire year.

RW threw his head back and roared with laughter. For the first time in…hell, he couldn't remember when…tears of laughter streamed down his face.

Indignantly, Claire stood. "It's not funny. Do you see what's in my glass? The health department will shut Jeffrey's restaurant down for this sort of negligence. I'm going to have a talk with the chef."

"Sit down," he ordered, wiping his eyes. "The chef is Jeffrey's wife."

She sat slowly. "My daughter-in-law did this to me? Why?"

RW shrugged. "She heard about the time you locked Jeffrey in the shed, Claire. Expect a night getting close and personal with your toilet bowl."

"She wouldn't poison me." Claire pushed her plate away just in case. "The shed thing wasn't my fault. The servants were supposed to let him out."

"That's crap. It was your fault and mine, too. I was so wrapped up in my own personal hell that I couldn't see what was happening in yours. Our kids deserved better parents than us, Claire. You deserved a better man. I'm sorry."

She cocked her head. "I've never heard you apologize before. Or laugh like you just did. You've changed."

"I'm working on it."

"I can see that. Don't change too much." Her gaze traveled over his tanned, muscular arms. "You're a good-looking man. Strong, rich, sexy. You're fine the way you are."

"You don't know me anymore."

"What do you mean? I married you and had your three children. I know you."

"I'm not the man you married. You left that guy for dead a decade ago. With good reason. I'm not an angry, despicable sap anymore. I…I woke up."

"You woke up? What does that mean?"

How could he explain it? He'd suffered from depression for most of his life. Deep down he'd known he needed help, but his parents had said that Harpers didn't have *those* problems. Claire must've known he was ill too, but she pretended the despair that overtook him—sometimes so debilitating that he locked himself in a dark room for days—was normal behavior.

She'd put up with the way he treated people. He'd been an ass, not because he wanted to be, but because he didn't know how to interact, to connect, when he hurt so much. Hell, running a multibillion-dollar company was far easier than connecting on a deeper level with the people he loved.

He'd closed off his feelings to survive. The only emotion that seeped out occasionally? Anger. Matt had been the only one who stood up to him, taking the rage that RW fought to control, shielding the rest of the family from RW's outbursts. His son shouldn't have had to live that way. None of them should've.

After a while, RW had reached a breaking point. Why take his next breath when no one cared if he did? His kids hated him. Claire wished him dead—that's what she screamed at him more than once—and he didn't care anymore. Ten years ago, he'd sent the kids away so he couldn't hurt them anymore and he quit life.

Or he tried to.

By some miracle he never deserved, a beautiful woman rescued him. She'd said he had a mental illness. If the wound had been in his leg, would he have let it fester and rot without treatment? she'd asked. No. So why be ashamed of the pain in his psyche?

Gentle, kind and strong, Angel became his therapist as he started the arduous process of healing his mind. Feelings, like colors of the sunset and sweetness on a tropical breeze, flooded his senses. He wanted to survive. No, more than that—he wanted to be happy.

Angel told him happiness was achievable if he followed her three rules: *seek redemption, make amends, forgive yourself.* The first two were going to take a lifetime to achieve, since he'd hurt so many people. He didn't deserve forgiveness.

But even though he was undeserving, he sought redemption anyway.

And he fell in love with Angel.

For the first time in his life, he had a purpose.

He woke up.

Claire would never understand. She turned her light brown eyes on him and twirled a platinum-blond curl around her finger. "Things weren't always bad between us."

"They weren't good enough. I know the difference now. I don't intend to ever settle again. How about you? Don't you want to feel joy? Happiness? Love?"

It was her turn to laugh, but there was more spite than humor in it. "What has gotten into you? You really think a guy like you can fall in love? When will you have time for it?"

His mood darkened. "Why are you here?"

"I want what's mine." She leaned over the table. Her stature was fiercely determined, but something else, too. Desperation. "The kids are back and you are better. Plunder Cove is where we all belong. Together."

He leaned over, too. "No. Go home, Claire. I've found someone else and I'm going to marry her, if she'll accept me."

He didn't tell her that he had no idea where Angel was at the moment.

"Polygamy is a crime, sweetheart," she said with a wicked smile. "Or have you forgotten? I didn't sign your divorce papers."

"Damn it, Claire! Enough. Sign the divorce papers, take your money, hop on that broom of yours and fly back to Santa Monica."

"Now, *that's* the man I remember." Crossing her arms, she sat back. She seemed rooted to the chair and was decidedly not leaving.

"This is my home," he said, "passed down from my family. Mine. Understand me? Be happy with the money I've given you the last ten years and get on with your life. Leave me the hell alone."

Without yelling or throwing anything, RW got up and walked away. He was surprised at how steady and sure of himself he felt.

He picked up his cell phone. "Robert, bring the Bugatti around to the side. It's time to go."

Claire would eventually sign those papers. He had no doubt. He needed to move on to the next item on his agenda.

He was sneaking off to a quiet town on the coast, far away from prying eyes. If all went as planned, he'd be back before his kids knew he'd left Plunder Cove. If they realized he'd overstated the extent of his illness this morning to sneak out, he'd have some explaining to do.

He couldn't drag his children into the danger surrounding Angel. He was expendable. Hell, he was living on borrowed time already. But the woman who'd saved his life needed him to save hers.

She'd been running from a Colombian gang of murderers and drug dealers for years, barely staying one step ahead of them. She'd been hiding in his home under an assumed name all this time. But when the gang came to his home, searching for her a few months ago, Angel fled to protect him.

She thought she'd be able to hide from the gang, from him, but he had resources she couldn't imagine.

Enough was enough. He'd do whatever he could to force Cuchillo and his gang to their knees and bring Angel home.

Even if it meant sacrificing himself as bait.

# Three

Chloe was about to combust or squeal or any number of things that would not be the least bit professional. Instead she quickly went down to the restaurant to talk to her sister-in-law.

She found Michele in the kitchen, her arms coated with flour as she kneaded pasta dough.

"You're here!" Chloe said.

"Where else would I be? Oh! How's it going with Mr. Dreamy Eyes?" Michele asked with a smile.

"He's so handsome…and that voice, the accent, oh, my God. He turns me to mush." Chloe closed her eyes and took a deep breath. "Complete idiotic mush. Mind if I pace a little? I grumble better when I'm moving."

"Grumble? Why aren't you ecstatic? You get to spend all week with him."

"It's not him—it's me."

"Have at it." Michele motioned to the floor. "Just don't slam anything around. I've got cake rising in the oven."

"I'm not my mother. I don't slam things." Chloe paced quietly, making sure not to stomp.

"Hey, speaking of the wicked witch…" Michele glanced over her shoulder and lowered her voice. "I messed with her a little earlier—not bad, just enough to teach her she's not welcome in my restaurant, *our* restaurant. She doesn't get a free pass after what she did to Jeff."

Chloe blinked. "Mom's still in Plunder Cove?"

Michele whispered, "Yeah. She met your dad for a late lunch. Weird, huh?"

*Weird* didn't begin to describe it. "Did she throw dishes, wine bottles? Did my dad toss her out?"

Goodness, if her parents started fighting while Nicolas was here, the deal for the show would be off.

"Not at all. They talked quietly. Civilly. Then your dad left before she did."

In the Harper household, civil parents didn't make sense. What were they up to? Chloe stopped walking in circles at the counter, where Michele was pounding the dough. "Can I do that?"

"You want to knead my dough?"

"Can I beat it a little, too?"

"Sure." Michele stepped back. "Wash up and you can knead away. Want to tell me why you want to punch dough?"

Chloe dried her hands and began kneading. "The

guy who inspired me to play the guitar is upstairs. In my house. Nicky M! And holy moly, he looks so good. I can't even begin to describe how well his butt fills out those slacks. But I'm representing the resort in this deal. I shouldn't be thinking about his anatomy!"

"But you are." Michele smiled wickedly.

*Well, yeah.* "You'd think I'd use this opportunity to—I don't know—ask him how he comes up with his perfect rhythm. Or ask about the inspiration behind his lyrics in 'Baby, Come After Me.' I have this amazing chance to learn about lyrics and music from a master. Instead of asking intelligent questions, I could barely put more than two sentences together. What's the matter with me?

"You have a right to be flustered. It's Nicky M."

There was that. Her crush aside, he'd been her inspiration for continuing to sing and play the guitar in her off time. Her parents had made it clear that being a singer wasn't her true calling, but it made her happy. Nicky M had given her that.

"I don't get starstruck. I got over that nonsense working at my yoga studio in Hollywood. Directors, big-name stars, models—they're just people. I dated enough of those guys to know that they're just looking for happiness and love like the rest of us. And quite a few of them are…" *As broken as I am.* She kneaded that dough until her hands hurt. "Lost. Hollywood ruins people. Star power doesn't have any effect on me."

"But Mr. Dreamy Eyes does?"

"Oh, gosh, yes." Chloe pressed a hand to her heart, leaving a handprint of flour on her blouse. "Maybe his eyes have hypnotized me. Yep. That's my story and I'm sticking to it."

Michele handed her a glass of wine, which Chloe waved off. "Wait, no alcohol either? I get giving up meat, but no wine? That's just…uh-uh. No way."

Chloe shrugged. "I'm trying to live better. Clean. Healthy." *Trying to learn to love myself.*

"I totally get it about Nicky M. If Gordon Ramsay came to hang out in my kitchen for a week, I'd probably accidentally cut off my hand or set the place on fire. Nicky M is yummy. Stop beating yourself up. You'll be fine once you relax."

Chloe poured herself a glass of water and took a long sip. "How do I relax? I can barely look at him without losing all rational sense."

"Hmm. That's an interesting dilemma since it's up to you to get him to sign the contract for filming his show here. I handle the food, and Jeff can only do so much. You have to sell it."

"Super. More pressure. You're not helping, Michele."

Michele smiled. "Sorry. Maybe you just need to find a way to work out your nerves. I cook when I'm stressed or, you know, have my way with your brother."

Chloe scrunched up her nose at that comment, even though she was thrilled Michele and Jeff were so deeply in love. That's all she ever wanted for her brothers, their happiness. She was working on her father's happiness next. RW and Angel were good together, even if Dad hadn't figured it out yet.

"Hey, that's it." Michele snapped her fingers and a puff of flour rose into the air. "You should kiss Nicky

M and get that nervousness out of your system. That's what I did the first time I cooked for your brother."

"Right. Just walk up and kiss a legend." What if his kisses didn't compare to her fantasy? Or worse. What if they were better? She'd be ruined for life.

"I don't mean assault the guy. Do what feels right for both of you. Jeff said Nicky M seemed to be into you."

Chloe's jaw dropped. "When did he notice *that*?"

Michele shrugged. "Men can feel the vibe, too."

Chloe shook her head. "Nicolas just got out of that train wreck of a relationship with supermodel Lila what's-her-name. He's not ready for anything else. And if I misread the situation…" It would be a disaster. She'd fail at getting the contract, fail at finally doing something right for her family. "Nope, nope, nope. Kissing Nicolas is not a good idea."

Michele cocked her head. "Or what if you're not misreading the situation? What if you're judging your feelings and his perfectly? It could be a really great thing, Chloe. I'm all for following your dreams. If I hadn't gone for mine, I wouldn't be here right now. You don't always get a second chance to make your dreams come true."

"I can't. I shouldn't. No, definitely not." Chloe could hear the disappointment in her own voice.

She needed to get this deal, for herself and for her family. But more than that, she'd meant it when she'd sworn off men. She'd spent too much time losing herself in men, in dating, in sex. She needed time to find herself, especially now that she was back in Plunder Cove.

Yet part of her knew that Michele was right. There

weren't always second chances to live in the moment. And a big part of her really, *really*, wanted to indulge in this moment with Nicolas.

That flicker of attraction he'd talked about? It was a raging wildfire inside her.

"And yet you want to," Michele said, reading what Chloe wasn't saying.

"Well, *yeah*."

Michele laughed. "Then if you get the opportunity and he's into it, go for it. When was the last time you got hot and heavy anyway?"

"Hot and heavy?"

"You know. Being with a man you want to shave your legs for."

"Let me think…" Chloe squeezed the dough in her fist. Should she tell her sister-in-law why she'd stopped dating? Would Michele understand?

"If you have to think that hard, it's been too long," Michele said with a laugh.

"I'm not, uh, dating right now. To find spiritual happiness, I need to find myself first. Loving who I am will help me find true love."

With her hand on her hip, Michele blew her bangs out of her eyes. "Seriously? No men? At all?"

"Something has to change," Chloe said quietly. She'd spent her life wishing someone, anyone, would love her. She'd been kicked out of the mansion when she was fourteen years old. Living with her mother had been difficult, to say the least. She hadn't heard from her brothers or father until recently, and her heart was still aching with desperation to keep them all close.

Michele's face softened. "Your life is changing. You're here, you're part of the family. You aren't alone anymore, Chloe."

Chloe's eyes welled. "I don't want to lose my family again."

"You won't, hon. I understand trying to better yourself—I do—but you're going to let your spiritual journey keep you from the man of your dreams? What if *he* is the love you should be with and you let him slip through your hands? And aren't you always the one saying you should appreciate every moment in life? You might not get this chance again."

Chloe chewed her lip. There was that. "I'm nothing like the women he usually dates."

"So? Maybe he wants a change, too."

"Nicky, uh, *Nicolas* did ask me to join him for dinner. A business dinner. If I thought he'd be into me—"

"You'd go for it?" Michele nudged her with her shoulder. "Do it!"

Should Chloe put her spiritual quest on hold so she could live out a fantasy? "Maybe."

Michele rolled her eyes. "You Harpers are so darn stubborn. Just go with your passions, Chloe. Let yourself breathe."

Chloe grinned. Michele had used one of the mantras Chloe had become famous for when teaching yoga to the stars. "You're a Harper now, too," she told her sister-in-law.

"And Jeff would tell you that I can be pretty stubborn myself. Use the strength you have and trust yourself."

Trust herself with a man she'd fantasized about her

whole life? And at the same time not mess up the contract her dad wanted her to secure? Her family was depending on her to get this right.

The whole situation sounded dangerous.

But more than anything, she wanted to breathe.

She kissed Michele's cheek. "Thanks for the pep talk. See you at seven. Make sure everything is perfect for dinner."

"Nice. Thanks for stressing *me* out now," Michele grumbled.

Chloe just waved as she left to find the man of her dreams.

Nicolas finished up his fifth phone call in the last few hours. He took out his laptop and checked his emails. He pressed the ache between his eyes. There were 120 music videos from potential candidates waiting for him that had been sent to him by his assistant, who had already waded through thousands of applicants. Putting on his headphones, he sat on the bed and viewed five of them. One kid was a standout, but the others were not even close. He put those four into the Do Not Call Back folder. Only 115 more to wade through.

This was a grueling process. He hated to shatter dreams, but only ten could be chosen for the show, and they had to be the best of the best. Rolling the tension out of his tight neck and shoulders, he stood and popped his spine. It had been a long day.

He cast his gaze longingly at the guitar he'd brought with him just in case the music returned to him. Nothing. It sat silently challenging him to write and play something worthwhile. Instead he went to the full re-frigerator in the kitchen, grabbed a beer, and went out onto his private patio for fresh air. The penthouse suite that Harper had put him in was full of amenities. He had everything he could ask for except a warm woman in his bed. He didn't sleep alone very often, especially not in a hotel room. He'd have to rectify that situation.

He sipped his beer and enjoyed the view from his balcony. The sinking sun had painted the sky in golden strokes. Warm breezes danced in the palm trees on the beach and lifted tiny white peaks on the Pacific. His gaze meandered back from the sea, up the grassy pas-tures and settled on a garden below his window.

The last rays of the sun lit a figure moving in the gar-den. He'd recognize that blond braid anywhere.

*Chloe.*

She wore tight purple-and-white-floral pants and a white T-shirt. Her clothes accentuated her awe-inspiring figure.

Was she dancing? He sipped his beer and watched. No, stretching. But nothing like the hamstring stretches he did before and after his runs. This was fluid, intense and beautiful. She was like a panther—flexible and strong. When she bent over and pressed her hands on the ground, her sweet ass pointed straight at him. The sight stirred him up.

Exhausted to erect in twenty seconds. A new per-sonal record.

The only sound he could hear was a mocking bird, the waves and the whisper of the wind through the trees. Still, she moved to her own beat, her internal rhythm, and became the personification of a melody. Something deep inside him pulsed, too.

Chloe lifted her long arms over her head and sat on an invisible chair. Nice, strong glutes. He doubted he would be able to hold a pose like that for so long. She rose up and went into a graceful lunge, one arm stretched in front, the other behind her. Straight lines like a warrior goddess. Bendy as a wet reed. She reached, squatted and arched her back. Even though she didn't know he was watching, Chloe seemed to be a woman on a single mission to drive him wild.

Every move and every hold was like a dance. Like sex. Who knew yoga could be so hot?

Before that moment he hadn't had the slightest interest in yoga because Tony Ricci, his former agent-turned-best-friend, had warned him against it. Tony'd had a bad experience with a yoga studio in LA. Supposedly the instructor was a man-eater.

Tony would probably tell Nicolas to stay away from Chloe too and keep his head on the show and his hands to himself. Most likely Tony would pull up a clip of Lila dumping Nicolas on camera. Nicolas didn't need any reminders.

Lila had used him, like so many others had, as a ladder to her success. He'd thought for a while that she'd be the one to fill the missing piece in his life. Lila was gorgeous, fun, sexy and had a pretty nice singing voice, too. Not amazing, but nice. He'd pulled all the connections he had to get his girlfriend the singing contract she'd asked for. How had she repaid him? By breaking up with him in front of tabloid cameras.

Lila didn't love him, but she adored his former drummer, Billy See. The two were engaged to be married and chose national television as the way to break the news. His buddy and girlfriend were off making music together.

And Nicolas was left alone, in silence.

*Merda.*

He watched Chloe reach for the sky.

Maybe Chloe was the music he needed to feel whole for a night.

# Four

Family was the most important thing in the world to Chloe. She'd lost her father and brothers once, when her father had sent them all away, and she'd sworn then that she'd do anything to get them back. By some miracle, they were all in Plunder Cove together again, working toward one goal—to make the Casa Larga Resort a success.

Jeff and Matt and their new brides had all given up their careers to come to Plunder Cove. The local town was invested in the new venture, too. Getting Nicolas to agree to Dad's plan was the next step in sealing everyone's future, and it was up to her to get it done.

She needed to wow him, which was about the place and had nothing to do with what she felt about him. Nothing. No matter how much his sexy Brazilian accent melted her, a Harper heiress did not throw herself at guests.

If she'd met Nicolas a year ago, she would've agreed to his dinner proposal without even questioning it and might have angled in for more already. In those days she'd been a serial-dater, a man-addict. At least that's what her mother had called her.

To that ridiculous statement, Chloe had rolled her eyes and replied, "That's a sexist comment, Mom. Men hit on me all the time at the yoga studio. Why shouldn't I say yes sometimes? It's not like I'm sleeping with all of them. Just having a little fun."

Besides, dancing, dinner and going to the movies kept Chloe from being home by herself. She'd been having a good time until the day she started crying over her morning matcha green tea because she was bitterly empty and alone. Though she'd glossed over it, she had never really recovered from her emotionally challenging childhood, and she still longed for stability and someone to love her.

Unable to shake the depression, she'd flown to Rishikesh, India, to her old yoga masters for a spiritual tune-up. She was surprised when they told her that her chakras were blocked. How had that happened? She was a yoga instructor who helped her students tap into the vibration from the centers in their own bodies, and yet hers was clearly not functioning properly. The chakra most damaged was her sacral chakra—the center for her emotions, creativity and sexuality.

Men were her shields for her loneliness and bandages to her wounded heart. When she was with a man, she didn't have time to sit quietly with herself and work through the abuse she'd lived through as a child. She used guys to keep from feeling and experiencing her own life. If she didn't correct the problem, her teachers told her, she would lose herself.

Oh, God. Mom was right.

The best way to fix the problem was to stop dating altogether until she was happy with who she was. "Go work on Chloe," her teachers had said. "Find her, love her and allow the light of the universe to open up for her."

Far easier said than done. She'd been on a self-discovery journey for over a year now and still wasn't satisfied with who she was. Coming to Plunder Cove was both helping—since she got to be with her family again—and dredging up past heartaches…because she got to be with her family again. It was a gut-twisting journey, each day full of baby steps forward and slinks backward.

Would she ever truly be happy? She had a terrifying feeling she'd never be a good girlfriend, let alone a wife or mother until she figured it out. She'd stood hip-deep in the holy waters of the Ganges and swore to herself that she would be a better person before she gave herself to anyone else.

For the first time since that day, keeping her promise was tough.

Remembering the casually sexy grin Nicolas gave her as he leaned against the door frame made her fan herself again. A year and a half ago she might've kissed Nicolas right then to steal back a little of her lost innocence. Today she knew she couldn't use him like that. He was the poster boy of her childhood dreams, but he was also a real man with real feelings—not a drug to ease her heartaches. Plus, he was going through his own issues after a public breakup with Lila what's-her-name. Why complicate things for both of them?

But oh, man, how that handsome Nicolas made her want to backslide straight into his arms.

Chloe shaved her legs.

There was a soft rap on his door at seven o'clock on the dot.

"*Boa noite*, Chloe," Nicolas said as he opened it.

She pressed her hand to her chest and sighed. "That never gets old. You could talk Portuguese to me all day. I wouldn't understand, but I do love to hear it."

He grinned and filed that tidbit away for a later time.

Chloe's hair was in a bun, with a few loose golden waves framing her face. She wore no makeup except lip gloss. The look was perfect. He preferred kissing skin over caked-on powder. He longed to see if the light pink gloss coating her lips was flavored.

"Are you ready?" Chloe asked, her voice breathy again.

She stood before him in a pale sleeveless blue dress with a deep V-neckline. A gold chain dipped into the valley between her breasts. Those toned arms that had recently held her body in a perfect plank glowed as if they'd been soaped and moisturized. In order to quell the urge to run his hands over her skin, he shoved his hands into his pockets.

"I am. You look gorgeous."

Her gaze took a nice stroll down his body and back up. "You do, too."

He liked the sound of that.

"Do I need a jacket for the restaurant?" He was wearing his tan slacks and black short-sleeve shirt.

She shook her head. "No, but you might want to bring one in case it gets chilly. I was hoping we could take an evening stroll. There are a few things I would love for you to see at night."

He cocked his eyebrow. What did Miss Chloe want to show him? "I'm all yours."

The blush crept up her neck and her lips parted. No sound came out.

He held out his arm. "Shall we?"

She hesitated for a split second and then hooked her arm with his. "Absolutely."

They went outside and down a winding torchlit path. The night air was cooling off quickly and the breeze danced in Chloe's hair. He tucked one of the loose strands behind her ear.

His touch seemed to give her a shiver. *File that away, too.*

"We're here," she said softly.

He could smell steak coming from inside, but the wood-and-glass two-story building didn't look like any restaurant he'd ever seen. "It's shaped like a…ship?"

"A pirate ship. Do you know the history of Plunder Cove?" She led him inside. "This property used to be a Spanish adobe on a land grant purchased back in the 1800s." She paused. "By the pirate Harpers."

He opened the glass door for her. "RW's ancestors were pirates?"

"That's the legend."

He knew all about legends. Truth and lies were told to keep the stories alive and certain men on top of the heap. What were Chloe's legends? He longed to hear them all.

A hostess called out, "Welcome, Mr. Medeiros. We're happy to have you here. Your table is ready."

They sat in a private alcove next to the window. The ocean view was expansive. It would be a great place to sit and watch the sun come up, especially after a night of lovemaking.

They ordered—him the Wagyu steak and lobster, her something vegetarian.

He made a face. "You don't eat meat?"

"Fish occasionally. Eggs sometimes."

He shook his head. "No idea how you live that way."

"It's a choice that's right for me."

A bottle of wine and a basket of fresh, steaming bread arrived.

"I saw you doing yoga in the garden," he said. "You looked…" He offered the basket of bread to her while searching for the right adjective. *Super hot* didn't seem quite appropriate from a guy who was spying on her while she stretched. "Flexible."

"Do you practice yoga? I teach a class in the garden tomorrow morning, as the sun comes up. You could join us." Interest lifted the notes in her voice.

"Me?" he chuckled. "Ah, no."

He took a sip of his wine. It was the best pinot he'd ever tasted.

"I could show you a few things, help ease that tension in your shoulders." She motioned toward him with her bread roll. "And your jaw. If you don't mind me saying so, it looks like you chew nails."

She could see he was tense from across the table? "No nails. Just a lot going on." He forced his shoulders to relax as he drank his wine.

"I know," she said softly.

He looked up from his glass. *Droga*. He'd been thinking about all the work he still had to do for the show, but the wisdom in those blue eyes and a soft, sympathetic expression made him believe she was thinking about his public love life. Or the explosion of it. Had she read all the damning details about his breakup? What a way to ruin the mood.

"How long have you been doing yoga?" he asked, changing the subject.

"Since I was fourteen. It saved my life."

He frowned. "Yoga?" He'd always heard it was some sort of mumbo-jumbo thing. At least that's what Tony had told him after he'd gotten dumped by a yoga instructor.

"Growing up as a Harper was hard. Very hard." She sucked in a breath and blew it out with force. "Past history. I won't bore you with the details."

He was surprised by the tears welling in her eyes. He reached out and touched her hand. "You can tell me about it. I'm a good listener." He wasn't—not always—but tonight he wanted to hear her story.

Her gaze met his. A large tear dropped off her lashes. "Maybe later...or never. Probably never." She shrugged. "Why ruin this moment with Nicky M?" She curled her hand around his and squeezed. Electric currents passed between their hands, and for a moment they just looked at one another.

"Nicolas," he corrected. "I'm not that teenager anymore. Sometimes it feels like I never was."

"I understand that. We all grow up, right? And move on."

"Sometimes there is no other option." He told himself the life he had now—wealthier than he could have imagined, the provider for his family—was enough. What did it matter that the poetry in his life was gone?

The waiter brought the appetizers, and Chloe pulled her hand away from his. A chill settled over him. Nicolas looked around to see if a window had been opened. No air moved in the restaurant. The absence of Chloe's warm skin on his had produced the chill. He'd never had such a reaction from holding a woman's hand before.

"I had to grow up and figure out some way to take control of my life. As a kid, I had no control of anything. I went with my mother to India. She hated it, but I found spiritual peace. Meditation and practicing yoga were worlds away from the lessons I'd learned in Hollywood. Polar opposites, in fact."

That surprised him. "You lived in Hollywood? Why have we not met before?"

She laughed. "We travel in different circles, Nicolas."

He really liked the sound of her laughter. "We need to rectify that situation immediately."

She sipped her glass of water. He noticed she hadn't touched the wine he'd poured for her. "I moved here because I couldn't stand the fakeness. The superficiality."

"Ah, you were an actress. Hollywood can be brutal for people starting out in the film industry."

"Good guess, but me, an actress?" She snorted. "Perform in front of cameras? Are you crazy? Well, yeah, I guess you are, Mr. Singer. I was a private yoga instructor with ten students at a time at most. No cameras. No squealing fans."

It was his turn to laugh. "I might have squealed when you did some of those stretches. You are very good. How do you move your body like that?"

"Practice. I can teach you some of those stretches."

"What would it take to convince you to go back to Hollywood?" he surprised himself by asking. Even more startling? He meant it. He wanted to see Chloe in her element, lifting that sweet backside in the air again. "I might want to try yoga. If you'd be my teacher."

"That place nearly destroyed me." There was a flash of something like pain in her eyes. "It crushed my spirit."

"That surprises me. You seem strong, calm, normal."

"I've been working on it. Coming home to be with my family was exactly what I needed. I won't go back to LA."

He'd be lying if he said he wasn't disappointed. "If I've learned one thing in the music industry, it is to never say never."

The entrées arrived. His steak cut like butter, and their conversation was smooth and flowing. Nicolas enjoyed the dinner even more as Chloe relaxed. It was fun when she was starstruck and tongue-tied around him, but this was better—spending the evening with an intelligent, insightful date.

"My spinach raviolis are sinfully good," Chloe said. "One of the things I've learned from my yoga practice—take your time to enjoy all the good things in life. Moment by moment."

She took a bite of her pasta and closed her eyes to savor the taste. Her bottom lip was wet with the light lemon-and-olive-oil sauce. The tip of her pink tongue touched the corner of her mouth, slowly getting every last drop. His fork stopped midair. He enjoyed Italian food, but he'd never been so turned on by seeing a woman eat raviolis. Pasta had never made him hard before.

Slowly she opened her eyes. Her cheeks pinked. Did she see the sexual hunger in his expression?

"You try it," she said softly, giving him a bite of her ravioli. "Close your eyes and describe what you taste."

"I'd rather watch you. You are sexy when you eat. Makes me think of how your lips would taste right now." His voice was low and sounded dirty. Chloe was turning him into a voyeur. He liked it.

Her response wasn't verbal. Her eyes widened and the pupils went dark. Slowly she inhaled through parted lips. He watched her beautiful breasts rise and fall. He liked that, too.

"Careful, Nicolas, or you'll make me break a promise to myself." Her cheeks seemed heated.

"What promise?"

Her gaze bore into his. "To keep my hands and lips off you."

"How can I convince you to break that promise? Over and over again."

Her mouth opened but the waiter stepped up to the table, interrupting the moment. "More water?"

"Yes, please," Chloe's voice was hoarse. He imagined her saying that to him, later in his room. Maybe she'd drop the *please* and add his name. Maybe she wouldn't say anything when she grabbed him and bruised his lips.

As the waiter poured water for both of them, Chloe downed half the glass, cleared her throat and changed the topic. "I've planned a few adventures to help you get to know Plunder Cove. Is there anything special you'd like to do while you are here?"

Nicolas couldn't keep his lips from twitching. The only special adventure he'd like to do was sitting across the table from him. And he'd like to do more than one thing with her. He had never met anyone quite like Chloe—pretty, genuine, unique, and he'd already seen how flexible she was. His imagination heated up.

He waited for the waiter to leave and then he leaned forward and said nice and low, "I'm sure you and I can figure something out."

"Nicolas..."

"Yes, sexy?"

She bit her lip. Her right hand curled in, gripping

the tablecloth and releasing. Was that how she gripped the sheets during sex? Yes, she was on the same page. She made a strange sound in the back of her throat and choked. Then she grabbed her wineglass and drank it dry.

"More?" He held up the bottle.

She coughed one more time. "Sorry. I never expected to hear my teenage dream call me that. It's a little overwhelming."

"Sexy?" He poured. "I'm just a man. And you are a very desirable woman. Two people who can make one another very happy."

"It's not that simple. I'm on the job and you are—" she let out breath "—you are my Nicky M."

He smiled. He liked the way she wanted to possess him. "I can be yours tonight, in the flesh. Let me make all your dreams come true. Say yes."

She toyed with her wineglass, her blue eyes capturing the candlelight. "And how would you know what all my dreams are?"

"Easy. You will whisper them to me. One by one. I'll make them happen."

She chuckled. "Do those lines work with supermodels?"

He lifted his palms. "*Claro*. Practice makes perfect, just like yoga."

"Man, oh, man. I'd better change the subject before I get myself into trouble."

"Trouble can be fun."

"Not when you're running away from it. I've spent

years trying to clean up the mess in my life. And I'm still...not there yet."

There it was again—the flash of pain in her eyes.

He frowned. What had happened to her? He knew all about messes. His life was littered with them. Instead of fixing them, he usually left them behind as fast as he could. Some things were just too big to change. But for the first time in a long time, he wanted to help someone who wasn't in the industry. A real person with regular problems. And kissable lips.

"Is there anything I can do to help?"

She cocked her head, studying him, and then she shook her head. "As lovely as that sounds...no, I've fallen into that trap before and it just makes things tougher. I learned the hard way that I let men be my crutches, but at some point I have to do the work and heal my own wounds. This is on me. I have to fix me by myself."

"Wounds?" The waiter showed up again before he could get Chloe to explain. "Hey, *homem*. Can I pay you to take a hike and leave us alone for a while?"

The waiter blinked. "Uh, sorry. I didn't mean to interrupt. The chef would like you to try her signature dessert. Two spoons?" Between them, the waiter placed a decadent tower of tiramisu drizzled with dark bitter chocolate and sweet caramel. He then left the table quickly.

Chloe whispered. "It's the chef's better-than-sex tiramisu."

"Better than sex?" Nicolas shook his head. "You have been with the wrong men."

"No argument there," Chloe said.

*File that information away, too.*

He was already strategically planning where he would lick her and exactly where he'd suck. At the moment he didn't care about his reasons for being at this resort. He wanted to ease Chloe's wounds, or at least try. He was going in.

# Five

His gaze caused a blast of heat to melt her insides.

She shouldn't be thinking about his body on hers. No man was supposed to be under her sheets until she fulfilled her promise to herself. Her gaze traveled across his shirt, and before she could stop herself, she was imagining releasing each button. She hadn't felt like this in a long time, maybe never. Her body pulsed with need. Usually, she could stay away from a gorgeous guy, but Nicolas was different. She had a feeling that his lips were better than a delicious dessert and she wanted, needed, a taste.

"All right, Mr. Hot Stuff." She took his spoon, scooped up a large bite and swirled it around in the chocolaty sauce. "Now close your eyes and open your mouth."

His lips quirked. "I like a bossy woman who wants to feed me a sex dessert."

Her heart was pounding way too hard when he opened his mouth. He peeked at her through those dark lashes.

"All the way closed," she ordered. Her hand was not exactly steady when she touched his tongue with the treat. "Don't just taste. Feel. Listen. Take everything in. Savor the moment."

Chewing, he tipped his head back and moaned with pleasure. Wow, she felt that between her own legs. Resisting him was going to be the hardest test on her self-journey yet. Each minute with him made her want to indulge in him and forget for a moment about the promises she'd made.

"I taste chocolate, cinnamon, mascarpone cheese. Espresso, I think. And some spices I cannot quite recognize. As for what I hear…" He tilted his head, listening. "I can hear you breathing, your heart beating strong in your beautiful chest. There. You shifted in your chair, pressing your legs together. You are thinking about all those dreams you want me to make come true."

She gulped. How did he know *that*?

He opened his eyes. So damned cocky. And something else… Hopeful?

"Might be the case with all those supermodels you've dated, but I was thinking about taking a bite of that tiramisu." Her hoarse voice gave her away. She shifted in her chair again, trying, as he'd said, to quell the ache.

"Admit it, Chloe. Say you want me more than any dessert."

*Oh, heck, yeah.*

And that was the moment she decided to say yes.

When would she get the chance to kiss Nicky M if she didn't go for it now? When would she feel a desire like this again? Since she'd never felt anything like it before, she refused to let it pass her by. She might have used all of those other men to forget her own problems, but none of them had ever made her feel like this.

She dragged her finger through the chocolate sauce. "I like sweet-and-sticky things." She licked it off her finger. "About the promise…"

"Yeah?"

"If you really meant it…that you want me…"

"I did. I do."

She chewed her lip. "I'm considering breaking my promise. For tonight."

He grinned. "Best news I've heard all year." He pushed his chair out and helped her with hers. He curled her arm under his. "Come. Let's get out of here."

Chloe was shaking when he led her outside, pulling her along the torchlit path toward the garden. A lot had changed in a few short minutes. Her head was spinning. Was she really doing this? Could she have one hot, unforgettable night with her fantasy man?

She swallowed hard.

As if sensing her nerves, he stopped walking and faced her. His warm hands cupped her cheeks. She could feel the callouses. Those amazing, talented fingers were now setting her skin on fire.

"Do you want me, *minha gatinha*?" he asked, his

expression sincere. "You can say no. There won't be any hard feelings."

She swayed, melting from his heat. Want flooded her senses. The walls she'd carefully erected to insulate herself from her past crumbled beneath her desire for this man.

She rose up on her toes and kissed Nicolas Medeiros on his beautiful lips.

When he returned the kiss, his full lips were far more delicious than she'd ever imagined. She got lost in the taste of him, the heat pulsing through her, the pure bliss.

"Wow." She sighed.

He rubbed her cheek with the pad of his thumb. "Indeed, far better than tiramisu." He angled in for another.

Her heart was pounding and every cell in her body was begging for another kiss. It took all the willpower she could muster to put her hand on his chest and not rip open the buttons. She held him at arm's length. She couldn't afford to be kissing such an important *guest* here, where Dad or his staff could see her. "Let's go somewhere. A secret place."

"Ah." He leaned in close like he'd done when they were on the stairs. "I like Chloe's secrets."

She took his arm and led him through the back of the garden, past the fountain and under the low-hanging wisteria. As they passed, he reached up and plucked a purple flower and held it to his nose.

"*Santa Mãe*, that smells almost as good as you do."

He'd been smelling her? She was in deep trouble here. She was already craving another taste of his lips. She had the feeling that once she let herself truly enjoy him, she would be lost. Could she throw away all the work she'd done over the last year, improving herself, for one quick fling?

She shouldn't. She knew it.

But in this moment, she wanted to indulge in Nicolas and deal with the consequences later.

"This is it. Over here." She pulled him through a small opening between the hedges. "Be careful that the branches don't tear your clothes."

When they slipped out the other side, they were in one of Chloe's special spots—a small grassy meadow on the edge of the bluffs overlooking the Pacific Ocean. There were no clouds to block the legion of twinkling stars above them. The moon was a spotlight on the midnight blue sea. A breeze rolled across the water, lifting the tips of the waves and blowing the salty fragrance their way.

"I was thinking this spot would be good for the show. You could film a few of the contestants here, especially at sunset. It's an inspirational place. A good songwriting place."

He whistled soft and low. "What a view. The shape of the bay reminds me of the moon when it is barely a fingernail-slice in the sky."

God, his imagery was amazing. That's what she'd loved the most about his lyrics. "That's where the Harper pirates boldly dragged off all their booty. It's where we modern-day pirates boldly strip off..." She stopped herself. "We swim at night. The phosphorescence in the water is really amazing if you've never experienced it."

"Maybe later. When was the last time you brought a guy to this secret spot?"

She chuckled. "Never. It's been years since I've been here. I was always alone."

"Years?"

"Yeah. When my parents split up, Mom and I were kicked out of the mansion. But I used to come here all the time to escape the yelling inside. No one knew I was here. It's peaceful."

"Sounds like you had a tough childhood." He wrapped his arms around her like a blanket to shield the bad memories and tugged her back against his chest.

"I did. Sometimes I felt so alone and helpless."

He understood those feelings.

"You were the one who saved me," she said.

He tipped his head so he could see the side of her face. "How so?"

"When my parents screamed at each other and did terrible things, your music was there for me. I feel like I've known you my whole life—you just didn't know me."

"I wish I had known you then. I would've done my best to make you smile." He rubbed her shoulder. "My younger self would have tried to sneak a kiss or two then, too."

"My teenage self would've passed out if Nicky M's lips had touched hers."

"How about now?" He turned her in his arms and kissed her on the lips.

"Yep, the world is spinning. More, please." She wrapped her hands around his neck and pulled his lips to hers. He deepened the kiss and she felt like she was flying up and off the cliff. He shifted his stance so he could hold her tight to him. She relished the feel of him against her—his hard chest, muscular thighs and...*oh*. He was very hard everywhere.

She sucked in a breath.

"Chloe," he whispered into her ear, making shivers roll up her spine and into her scalp. "It's your call. We can go back to my room and make love all night. The rest of the world be damned." He pressed his lips against the shell of her ear. "No stress. No strings."

She sighed. "This won't have any impact on the contract or the show, right? Just one fun night."

He studied her for a long beat. "A fun, *sexy* night."

She held out her hand. "Deal."

He took her hand, turned it up and nibbled on the palm. Then he kissed a few fingers and sucked her thumb into his mouth as if she was the sweetest thing he'd ever tasted.

"Deal."

She was in way over her head.

# Six

He kissed her hard to seal their arrangement. Then he took her hand and led her back inside the mansion. No one was in the hallway. They were alone.

"Want anything to drink?" she asked. "I can get something from the cellar."

"Got any *cachaça*?"

"I don't know what that is."

"Most Americans don't. It's similar to rum and is used to make *caipirinha*, one of my favorite Brazilian drinks. How about bourbon, whiskey, tequila?"

She led him to a lounge chair. "Here. Sit and I'll go see what I can find."

"Wait." He hooked her wrist and pulled her closer. "Don't go."

The look she gave him spoke in sexy volumes. Passion darkened her light eyes and set the golden feathers aflame. She sucked in her bottom lip as if she could already feel his mouth on hers. She wanted him to kiss her. That made two of them.

He pulled her close. Hanging on, his hands around her waist, he dove in. She tasted better than *cachaça*. Chloe did not hold back. She ran her hands behind his neck, through his hair, and fastened his lips to hers. When he felt the pressure of her tongue against his lips, he opened up and let her in. She made an exquisite sound of pleasure. His tongue pushed hers back and he tasted as much as he could. Still, he couldn't get his fill.

He pressed her against the wall, caging her with his arms, wishing he could take her right there. He didn't want to think about what this meant or when it would end. He needed to feel. To drive both of them higher until her moans of delight became the music he couldn't create, let it fill his silent brain. He was desperate for release and peace.

With his eyes on hers, he slowly ran one hand over her throat, collarbone and chest until he found her breast. He cupped it through her clothes, enjoying the weight of it in his hand. God, she was perfect.

"I want you naked," he growled.

She was breathing fast. Her hands were on his ass. "Feeling is mutual."

They kissed and groped each other in the hallway like teenagers so hot for each other that they couldn't move toward his room. Or hers. He sucked her bottom lip and she cried out in his mouth.

There was a noise from down the hall and Chloe ripped her lips away from his. Her eyes were wild. "Oh, God. Is it my dad? He can't know about us. Come on, let's go."

She dragged him to his room, unlocked the door with her universal key and pulled him inside. He barely had a chance to register how badly she really didn't want her father to know about them. Her lips were on his throat and she was sighing in that way that made him hot. He didn't care who knew what at this point.

"Nicolas." Her lips moved against the cord of his neck. "There's something you should know."

"Another secret?"

"Sort of. It's more an admission. It's been a long time since I dated anyone. I'm probably rusty and not as practiced as the women you usually date. I'm especially not like your last supermodel. At all. I don't want you to be disappointed."

He ran his hand down her cheek. It was so damned soft. "My supermodel?"

"Tell me the truth." She tipped her head up and her eyes shimmered in the moonlight pouring through the window. Her gaze poured over his face, searching for… what? He hadn't lied to her. Did she think he would? "Do you want to sleep with me as a rebound? It's okay if you do, I understand revenge sex, or trying to forget her or…whatever this is. I just… I want to know."

Making love to this gorgeous woman would go a long way toward helping him block out what Lila and Billy had done to him. They'd destroyed his trust and friendship. He would never trust like that again. He'd been burned enough.

But none of that had anything to do with Chloe.

"I'm over Lila."

"Thank God." She let out a breath she'd been holding. "She was horrible. You deserve so much better. I'd never do what she did to you."

"Good." He nuzzled her neck. He wouldn't let anyone do that to him again. He was no fool. "I want you, Chloe. You're special, different, refreshingly honest. I don't care if you are rusty. I promise we will have a good time enjoying each other."

"You want me. Just as I am?"

"Hell, yes."

She hesitated and he wondered, not for the first time, why she had made that promise to herself not to touch him. And then she kissed him again and whispered against his lips, "Good."

He cupped her jaw. "Now my turn. I'm worried you'll be disappointed with me. I'm under a lot of pressure to live up to your fantasy."

She smiled and his heart did a funny, fluttering beat. "So, we're both under pressure, huh? What in the world are we going to do to release it?" She pressed her hand to the bulge in his pants.

"Careful, *mulher*." His voice was husky. "Keep breaking your promise like that and you're going to get into a whole lot of trouble."

Her eyes were hooded. "That's the plan. I'm going to get into as much trouble as I can tonight. Over and over. No regrets."

He was glad they were on the same page.

Nicolas didn't have female friends. With the exception of a few brief relationships, he mostly had quick hookups, which might last for a long weekend. If she didn't want to spend the night with him, he'd just as soon leave Plunder Cove and send someone else in his place to scope out the resort for the show. An entire week of sexual frustration was not part of the job description.

"I want you, Nicolas. Just as you are," she said as she ran her hands down his back.

He dove his hands into her hair and devoured her lips.

She unbuttoned his shirt. Her soft hands dipping inside the opening. "Please, I need to touch you."

He had no problem with that. He pulled the shirt off his shoulders and she inhaled in awe. If that didn't do his ego good, nothing would.

He stood before her, willing to go at whatever speed she needed or wanted. Her gaze traveled over him as if memorizing every inch of his skin. He couldn't remember anyone looking at him like that. She pressed her palms to his chest and slowly, tentatively touched his skin.

"So warm, muscular. My fantasies don't compare to this."

He grinned. "You can touch me all you want, *gata*."

"What happened here?" She fingered an old scar near his collarbone.

"Surfing accident when I was a kid."

Her eyes met his. "You surf? I didn't know that. I used to surf a lot."

"Me, too. I don't have much time for it anymore."

"Plunder Cove doesn't typically get big waves, but we can bodysurf while you're here."

"Naked?" he asked.

She looked up to see if he was kidding. He wasn't, if she was game. Her smile was wicked. "As long as no one sees us."

No one in general, or her family? She was a grown woman. Why was she so concerned about her family judging her? Or was she mostly worried about what they'd think if she was with him? He'd get to the bottom of it. Later.

Her fingers trailed over a rib and continued to trace his abs. "You are so beautiful. I can't believe I'm really touching you. It seems like a dream."

He tipped her chin up to look into her eyes. "You are the beautiful one, Chloe."

She pressed her lips to his chest in one long, intense kiss. She breathed in the smell of his skin, exhaling pleasure. No one had ever done that to him before.

Wrapping one arm around his back, she flattened the other hand over his heart as if trying to connect to the rapid beat. Wet, delicious kisses peppered his skin. She savored the taste of him as if he was her tiramisu. It was incredibly hot. He'd never been so turned on while keeping his pants and on. Chloe was amazingly sexy and hadn't taken anything off, which he wanted to fix immediately. She said she was rusty, but obviously knew her way around a man's body. He liked this slow, intense pace, but it was getting harder and harder to keep his racing hormones in check. He wanted to kiss her badly.

She lightly dragged her nails down his back. Goose bumps danced across his skin, rejoicing at her touch. When her hand cupped his ass, while her lips trailed wet kisses across his chest, he couldn't keep himself in check any longer.

"Chloe," he growled. "I want you naked." He pulled her to him, grabbed her ass and lifted her off the floor. "Now." He carried her to his bedroom.

He set her feet down next to his bed and sat on the mattress to watch her undress.

With her gaze on his, she unzipped her dress and let it drop to the floor. Her light blue bra and panties matched the dress and looked amazing on her skin. But he wanted them on the floor, too. Yesterday.

When she stepped out of her panties, he sucked in a breath. She was lean and sleek, with a narrow waist, taut core muscles and perfect breasts from years of practicing yoga. Nothing phony; no corrections needed.

"You are so damned beautiful." He rose to his feet, kicked his pants and briefs off and wrapped his arms around her. *"Linda,"* he mumbled with a kiss to her neck.

He ran his hand down her shoulder, her breast, her belly, her side and stopped on her amazing butt. All the while, her gaze was locked on his, her pupils dilated.

He sat back down on the bed and pulled her closer, pressing her legs wider until they were straddling his lap. He cupped her and ran his finger through her folds. "Tell me what you want, Chloe."

She gasped and closed her eyes. "You."

"Look at me."

Her eyes flew open.

"I'm no fantasy. Say what you want."

"You. To put that amazing mouth on me."

He grinned. He held on to her backside and placed a kiss right where she wanted it.

"Oh, God." She swayed.

"I've got you," he said before kissing her again. She squirmed in his arms. He licked and she started breathing heavily. He licked a few more times and she was panting. She sounded close. He really wanted to slow this down so she could savor every second, but he couldn't. He was close, too. He sucked.

She yelled out and collapsed into his arms.

He picked her up and laid her down on the bed.

"Don't move. I'll be right back." He went to grab a condom.

"Move?" she laughed. "With what bones?"

He put the condom on the pillow and stretched out beside her. She ran her hand over his chest, down his belly and gripped him.

"Mine," she said. "For tonight." She scooted down and put her mouth on him. Warm, wet heat engulfed him. She did something with her tongue that made him see stars. It was too good, too much.

"Hell, Chloe, I need to be inside you."

She took the condom, put it on him and then climbed on top. She was so wet. So hot. She rode him hard, fast.

As if desperate for release. But he didn't want this to end yet.

He gripped her hips and slowed her down. It was his turn to savor every moment. He sat up so he could reach her lips. He kissed her as he went deep, and pulled back slowly. He could feel her muscles tightening, hanging on, loving him on the inside, as he devoured her mouth. He wanted to touch her everywhere at once. To please her in every way.

Deep dive, slow retreat.

Her hips rocked with him, a perfect slow dance. Intensely intimate.

He went even slower this time. She moaned and bit her lip as he pulled back. The expression of pleasure on her face sent a shock wave to his balls. They were both panting now. She cupped his jaw and licked his lips, her hair draping his face, her blue eyes locked on to his. Emotions, raw and pure, flooded her expression. He'd never seen anything sexier. Had never been this connected with a woman.

Deep dive, slow retreat.

Her lips parted and a breathy moan came out. He felt it deep in his chest. This wasn't his style, this slow-motion, deeply connected love. It was emotional somehow in ways he couldn't quite figure out, but he liked it. He liked her. He wanted their night to be as good for her as it was for him. More than that. He didn't want it to end. For a few moments he could let himself hear the music in his soul. Feel that he deserved that look of awe on her face.

He rubbed her back, hips and smooth legs.

Deeper…

She moaned and gripped his shoulder. Waves of searing heat rolled through him. He held her hips and encouraged her to pick up the pace. And she rode him faster, faster, throwing her head back and arching her spine. His vision was filled with stars. He couldn't hang on much longer. She cried out and he joined her as they both sailed away in ecstasy.

# Seven

Nicolas tucked Chloe in close, his arm around her so he could touch her in as many places as possible as she slept. She was out like a light, softly snoring, completely satiated. He went to sleep with a smile on his face.

The dream started up quickly.

He was on a stage, getting ready to sing, but he didn't have a song. The audience booed him, calling him a loser. It was a repeat performance dream that he had at least once a month, only this time something was different. He wasn't alone. Chloe stood beside him with her hand in his.

She kissed him on the cheek and said, "Don't listen to them, Nicky. Be better."

He blinked at her. How?

She nodded at him like he knew the answer.

For her, he picked up his guitar and started to play. A wild melody poured out of him that was strong enough to vanquish the crowds and push back the despair. It was as brilliant and pure as Chloe's blue eyes, as intricately wound as her long braid.

The music was so real that his eyes opened. He wondered for a split second where he was. *Not my bed. Harper's home.*

He didn't linger on the thought, because he had to hurry and grab his guitar. He could still hear the chords of the melody, feel it pulsing through his blood. He got up quietly so as not to wake Chloe, took his guitar into the other room of his suite and closed the door behind him.

The first notes sprang from his fingers. He played the chords of the song from his dreams over and over again, trying to remember the rest. He couldn't quite grasp it. Still, he knew he was smiling as he strummed because miracles like this didn't happen to him anymore. He was flying. Joyful. For the first time in years, he was riffing on a new song that no one had heard before.

Chloe had opened a door inside him that had been bolted shut for too long. How had she done it? He'd only slept with her once, and yet he was dreaming about her. That never happened to him. She had touched him, maybe deeper than anyone ever had, and she had flipped one of his recurring nightmares into a song with real potential.

He played the chords again, faster, with more heart. The sound was unique and fresh. It reminded him of hope. Truth. Redemption.

Chloe.

* * *

It was early, probably around five o'clock in the morning, and Chloe was awake and gazing at Nicolas's face. God, he was gorgeous when he slept.

A stream of moonlight came through the window and highlighted a lock of his hair that had fallen across his forehead. How she longed to brush it off his brow, but she didn't dare move for fear she'd wake him. She stayed perfectly still and soaked him in. His jaw was relaxed. The stress lines above his nose were gone and his full lips parted slightly as he breathed in and out. The best part was that his arm was still wrapped around her as if he wanted to keep her. If he really did, she'd never move again. But that was crazy thinking. It was a one-night stand—nothing more. And she was the luckiest girl on the planet. The night had been magical. But it was only temporary because she needed to find herself.

Nicolas had kept his end of the bargain and loved her like she was special, important. He took her to heights she hadn't reached in a long time—maybe never before. She'd let herself go, while cherishing every moment. He was amazing. It was all a glorious memory to keep and replay like a movie or a song whenever she got lonely.

Like right now.

Even in his bed, while touching him, smelling his clean skin, studying his face like it was the last time, she felt bereft. Her heart beat was a solemn drumming in her chest. She knew herself well enough to know that the single night of bliss was going to come with consequences.

Because already she longed for more kisses and touching. More Nicolas.

*There is no more.*

She blinked hard on the burning sensation behind her eyes. Last night was a fantasy, pure and simple. Now he had to go back to being a guest at the resort, and it was time for her to be professional. To continue in her quest to find something that would last longer than just one night. Their secret deal was done. If she stuck around for the morning hellos, she'd only embarrass herself by wanting what she couldn't have. Best to get gone before any of the blubbering or begging started.

She slipped out of bed and tiptoed out the door. She made it to her own room without a single tear dropping and went to the bathroom to clean up. Somehow, she was going to pretend she hadn't had the best sex of her life with the man of her dreams. She would go teach her yoga class at 6:00 a.m. and act like nothing had happened between them. Like the world hadn't just tilted on its axis while she was in his arms.

For all she knew, nothing extraordinary had happened for him. Maybe it was just another Tuesday with some woman he'd forget by Friday.

She couldn't let that bother her. She wouldn't. She'd known going in that it was nothing more than a no-strings night. Now it was her job to show Nicolas around Plunder Cove and get him to fall in love with the place. Falling for her wasn't part of the plan. Her family depended on her. She could do this. Somehow.

After she got out of the shower, she found a note on

her bed from her dad. It was early and Dad had already stopped by? That couldn't be good.

"I want to talk to you," was all it said.

*Crapitty-crap-crap.* Did he know she'd spent the night with Nicolas? Was he going to think worse of her? Be angry? Tell her to go back to LA? Once she was ready to face the answer to those questions, Chloe knocked on the door to her father's study. Her palms were sweating.

"Enter," her father's voice called out from inside.

"Hey, Dad. Are you okay? It's early."

She stepped inside his library and immediately felt like the eleven-year-old girl who'd lost control of her bike and crashed into the Lamborghini, leaving an ugly scrape on the sports car.

RW Harper sat at his massive desk. He was writing on a large yellow tablet that he turned over when she stepped inside the room. She saw columns and notes as if he was weighing a pros and cons list.

"I can't sleep. Come in, sweetheart. There is something I want to talk to you about."

"Yeah, I know, Dad. It just sort of happened. I won't do it again. I promise."

He looked at her over his reading glasses. "This is about your mother. You need to convince her to leave Plunder Cove. She might listen to you. I want her gone before Angel comes home."

This wasn't about spending an outrageously hot night with a man she was supposed to be wooing as a Harper representative? Relief rushed into her limbs.

"Oh! You've heard from Angel. When is she coming back?"

Her dad's face was solemn. "No, I haven't heard from her, but I'm making arrangements to bring her back. I need her, Chloe. I'll do everything in my power to make her safe here."

"That's good, Dad. She should be here with you. You guys are great together."

"It's all her. She makes me a better man."

The conviction in his voice helped to cement her theory—Dad was falling in love with Angel. Did he know it yet? She studied him. He seemed thin, and his face showed signs of fatigue, but he wasn't as gray as he had been. His cheeks were slightly pink, like hers got when she was energized or embarrassed. More than that, she noticed an intensity to him. He wasn't depressed. His gaze was just as piercing as always. And that yellow notepad he had been writing on, the one he didn't want her to read, intrigued her.

Whatever he was planning must have something to do with how he was going to bring Angel home.

What was he up to?

"Your mother can't be hanging around here, Chloe. She needs to go back to Los Angeles."

"I'll talk to her, Dad, but you know Mom."

"Unfortunately, I do."

Claire Harper was a force to be reckoned with—a woman who did what she wanted and made life hell if you tried to stop her. Chloe wasn't sure why her mother hadn't left yet. Perhaps Mom wanted to see Jeff finish the resort. She was extremely proud of Jeff's accomplishments. Chloe crossed her fingers and hoped that was the reason Claire was still in Plunder Cove, and not anything more sinister.

"I'll try."

"Please, do what you can. I need Angel," RW said.

*Please?* RW Harper did not use that word very often. "I will." Chloe kissed his cheek. "Is there anything else I can do for you?"

"Just one, Chloe. Be careful," he said. He looked her in the eye and she saw a swirl of emotions. She was used to anger, disgust and intolerance on RW Harper's face, because during her childhood, that was all she'd seen. Since Angel had come into his life, though, Chloe had been surprised by how expressive her father's eyes could be. Her father was a different man than the one who'd broken her heart as a child. His transformation was strange and amazing all at once.

"I am, Dad. I won't let you down."

# Eight

Nicolas reached for her before he opened his eyes. His bed was empty. She'd left him before the sun came up? Women didn't usually run away from his bed so quickly. He usually walked them out and had his driver take them home. This was…unusual.

*What did you expect,* homem? *It was a one-night stand. You shook on it.*

Strangely, he felt sad about their deal. It was what he'd wanted last night, and yet he wasn't happy about it in the foggy haze of morning. The way Chloe made love—no, not made…*savored* love was inspiring. He'd never been with a woman who had touched him like she had. Would a second night be the same way? Did he have the right to ask her to extend their arrangement?

Probably not. She'd been clear about not wanting her

family to know about their attraction. He was going to have to act like Chloe Harper had not gotten under his skin.

Since he was awake and frustrated, he got out his laptop and immersed himself in his job. Like any other day.

After an hour of critiquing show contestants, Nicolas stretched his arms over his head and stood up. He needed a break. The singer-songwriters were all starting to blend together. Why couldn't these kids write something unique? Something that grabbed his heart, or gut, and wouldn't let go?

Perhaps it was because none of the artists had really lived yet. Storytelling required backstory, angst, a broken heart and devastating loss. He sighed. He'd had all of those things in spades by the time he was eleven. He didn't actually wish any of it on another kid.

Stretching his neck, he stepped out onto the balcony. The sun had just come up and the landscape was peaceful. He took in a deep breath and instead of inhaling the sweet smell of flowers or grass, he picked up a fragrance that reminded him of his childhood in Brazil—the sea. He longed to go for a swim.

*Naked. With Chloe.*

Down below, he saw her. She had a small class of about seven women, all stretching and reaching toward the sun. None of the seven women did the poses as well as Chloe. Nor looked as hot. He put his bathing suit on, determined to convince her to join him for an early-morning swim after her workout. Maybe once they got to the shore, they could strip their suits off.

He continued working until he heard her door close down the hall. Draping a towel around his neck, he knocked at her room. The pounding heartbeat in his chest surprised him. He felt like a teenager again, throwing rocks at his first girlfriend's window. The strangeness of the situation did not get past him. He was years and many girlfriends away from his first girl. Chloe was a sexy hookup—nothing more. And yet... his heart raced to see her again.

Chloe must have seen him through the peephole because her cheeks were already pink when she opened the door. Her face looked sparkly clean, as she wore no makeup. Her hair was in one long braid draped over her shoulder. Her pale blue tank top and yoga pants clung to every curve. He had to stop looking. His swim trunks were getting tighter by the moment.

"I'm not here to cause trouble," he said quickly.

Her gaze took a quick trip down his mostly naked body and popped back up again to his face. "As long as you're not here to cause trouble."

He couldn't help but smile. Discreetly, he wiped his damp palms on his towel. Chloe had quite an effect on him. He had to get a grip.

"The sun is shining, the sky is crystal blue and the water is wet. Come bodysurfing with me," he said.

She smiled and his pulse stilled. His chest warmed. How did she do that?

"Now?"

He shrugged. "Unless you have something else planned for us." He was hopeful their plans might involve dropping those yoga clothes to the floor.

"We were going to start with breakfast. Do you want to hit the waves first?"

He leaned against her door frame, crossed his arms casually and asked. "What's for breakfast?"

She swallowed loudly, as if she'd read his mind. He wanted to taste Chloe again. He could skip eggs and bacon and kiss her all morning instead.

"Whatever you're hungry for?" Her voice cracked.

He pushed off the door frame and moved closer. She smelled so good. "In that case I'm craving more of last night. You left before the sun came up. Why?"

Her eyes widened. "We had a deal. One night only."

To hell with that. He wanted heat, pressure…her. He caressed her cheek and marveled again at how soft her skin was. "I got robbed. Make it up to me." He took her hand in his and rubbed her palm. He'd promise her anything if she'd agree.

Her beautiful lips parted into a shocked O-shape. "We agreed—it was a casual, one-time thing."

It was supposed to be, but there was nothing casual about last night. Chloe had given him something special—herself. People didn't usually do that during hookups. They always kept something under a mask, protected, reserved. Chloe hadn't held anything back. She'd touched him as if they'd been lovers for years. No, better. As if they'd been *in love* for years. He had never experienced anything like it and he wanted more, needed more.

"Is that what you want? To put last night behind us?" his mouth asked, but his body was already humming with the ache to pull her into his arms. He was a little stunned by his growing need for her. She wasn't his usual type. Chloe was sincere, earthy, real. He'd never been with anyone like her.

She blinked. "I don't understand. You still want me?"

"Hell, yes." It came out as a growl. "Chloe, last night was one of the best I've ever—"

She grabbed the towel around his neck and pulled him close. He forgot what he was going to say when her lips melded to his. She was such a fantastic kisser. His tongue probed her sweet mouth, tasting minty toothpaste. His hands roamed over her skin as he tried to reacquaint himself with her curves and lean muscles. Heat engulfed him and he was instantly hard.

She pulled her lips away long enough to whisper, "Come inside." She guided him into her room and closed the door behind him.

He pressed her up against the wall. Lifting one of her legs, he wrapped it around him. She was so damned flexible. Gripping her hips, he moved her into the perfect position and kissed her hard. A hungry growl rumbled at the back of his throat.

She cupped his face with her hands and kissed as good as she got. She was hungry, too. He kissed her neck and peeled her tank top off her shoulders. Her bra beneath the tank was lacy and black, beautiful.

*"Beleza."* He kissed her soft skin from her collarbone down into her cleavage, and unlatched the bra, freeing two exquisite breasts. Not large, not small, but simply perfect. He cupped one while kissing the other.

Chloe moaned with pleasure. "More."

He sucked.

She arched her back and tipped her head back, breathing fast.

"Like that?" he asked.

She bit her lip and nodded.

"Say it, *gatinha*."

"More, Nicolas. Give me more." She pressed down against his erection, rolling her hips.

He liked that.

They moved together. Flying, dancing, a perfect melody of a sexy song. He took the other nipple into his mouth, playing with it, licking, teasing.

She gripped his head, holding him in place. He reached his hand into her yoga pants and was pleased to find her not wearing underwear. He cupped her and pressed his finger inside her wetness.

"Oh…feels so…oh…" She didn't finish the sentence. She rocked against his hand. Beautiful, wild and sexy beyond words.

He sucked her nipple while she rode him. Chloe cried out, coming undone. So unbelievably beautiful. He pulled her lips back to his and savored them.

"So? Can we extend our deal? Stay another night with me. The whole night this time."

She pressed her forehead to his and opened her eyes. "I swore to keep my hands off you. Now look at what I've done." She was playing it light, but there was a hint of something else in her voice… Sadness?

"Why did you make that promise?" He sat on her love seat and pulled her into his lap, curious.

She played with his hair. "I'm trying to focus on

making myself a better person before I lose myself in someone else."

"You seem pretty great to me."

Her bottom lip quivered. "I'm not great. You don't know what it's like to be a Harper. I've never been loved, Nicolas. Not ever. By anyone. I want what other people have, just once—to feel loved. Like I deserve it."

He was going to still that lip after she answered the next question. "Your family didn't love you?"

"My father sent us all away and I had no contact with any of them except my mother. And my mother…well, she doesn't show love."

He pressed a gentle kiss to both of her lips. "You deserve love, *gata*. You've had a run of bad luck. That's all. You don't need to change who you are for anyone."

She pressed her hand to his chest. Connecting with his heartbeat again. "You're amazing, Nicolas. I'm glad I got to know you."

He held out his hand. "Do we have another deal? I will prove to you that you are special the way you are. If things work out, we will have a whole week together. I promise that you are a better person than you believe you are. Let me show you how wonderful you are."

"And then? After the week is done?"

"I go back to Los Angeles and get ready for the show."

"Alone, again?" She petted his cheek. "Don't you want more in your life? I want so much for my life and relationships."

"Relationships don't last. All I want is here and now—you naked and me deep inside you." He was still hard and aching to feel her under him, or over him—he didn't care. He'd take her any way she'd let him.

She ran her finger over his bottom lip. "I want that, too. But I want the feeling to last. I've never had a long-term loving relationship, or anything real. At this time in my life, I need to set the bar to that level. Real love that lasts. Don't you want someone who—" her gaze was intense and sincere "—fills your dark spots?"

He thought he'd wanted that…once. He'd failed then and would fail again. He wasn't cut out to be anyone's lasting relationship. Even knowing he couldn't be that for Chloe, he wanted her for this short time.

"Long-lasting doesn't work for me. People take what they want and then everyone leaves…" He paused. "I will make you happy for the week, but I'm not your forever-after man, *gata*. I don't know how to be that guy."

Her gaze bored into his with such anguish and conflict that his heart melted, but he held his ground. He wouldn't lie to her. The next step would be up to her.

"Decide what you want, Chloe, and I'll give it to you. No questions, no pressure." He lifted her off his lap. "I'm going to take a quick shower and then we can meet for breakfast. Bodysurfing will have to come later. I'm starved."

# Nine

*Nicolas Medeiros wants me?*

She would have thought she was dreaming, except she was still jelly-legged from his wicked touch. The man had a way of making her come like no one else. A reckless, wanton ache between her legs made her want to race down the hall and be with Nicolas again. But something he said kept her feet rooted to her silk carpet.

*Everyone leaves.*

She knew exactly how that felt. How much of his sentiment related to his recent breakup? Chloe didn't know, but she'd never been one of those people who got what they needed and then walked away.

She wished she could be the one to show him what a long-term relationship looked like. Funny. She'd never had any sort of relationship herself, and maybe she still wasn't ready for one, but she knew she could love someone forever if she had the chance. That's why finding herself before dating anyone else had been so important to her.

But that was before Nicolas.

She could try to explain this belief in love to him, but he'd have to decide that he wanted it for himself.

She cared about him. She didn't want to be on his list of users and leavers. Staying away from him would be the best thing for both of them, no matter how fantastic his lips felt on her skin or what his hot gaze did to her insides.

But staying away was impossible, both personally and professionally.

How would she get her job done if she couldn't work with him? Nicolas was her job, the only assignment her family had given her. What would Dad say if she told him she couldn't do what he'd asked because she wanted Nicolas Medeiros more than any contract?

She groaned. What was she going to do?

*Wait. What was that?*

She opened her door, peeked her head into the hallway, and listened.

*Music.* Nicolas wasn't in the shower; he was riffing on his guitar in his room. The sound was both haunting and passionate.

Just like Nicolas.

Chloe's cell phone rang on her nightstand. She closed her door and saw Michele's caller ID on the screen as she answered.

"You'd better get down here," Michele whispered.

"Your mother is expecting me to feed her breakfast. Demanding, really. Please say I can kick her out on her skinny butt."

"No! Do not throw her out or she'll make a huge scene. I don't want Nicolas to see Mom's antics."

"Dreamy Eyes is not with you?" Michele asked coyly.

*Sadly, no.* "Tell Mom I'm coming. Get her a Bloody Mary and do not make small talk with her. Repeat— do not engage."

"Sounds like a crocodile," Michele mumbled before she hung up.

Chloe hastily changed into a white dress and hustled down to find her mother sitting at the same table where Chloe and Nicolas had sat the night before. It had the best view in the place. There was some light cloud cover over the water, but other than that it looked like it was going to be a gorgeous day.

"Chloe, darling. So glad you could join me for breakfast," Mom said. She kissed Chloe's cheek and whispered, "The chef is quite obnoxious. Don't know what Jeff sees in her."

"She's actually quite lovely." Chloe sat across from her mother. "What are you doing here, Mom?"

"I can't come have breakfast with my daughter?" Claire pouted.

"Sure. I could've met you somewhere, like say, Santa Monica? They have lots of nice restaurants on the Breakwater."

Claire sipped her Bloody Mary. "I was hoping I might run into your father. Can you call him? Ask him to join us?"

Chloe's jaw dropped. "You *want* Dad to join us. Why?"

"You and your thousand questions." Claire shook her head. "I might have missed your father. A little."

Chloe sat back in her chair. "How much alcohol is in that glass?"

"Hardly any." Claire fluffed her hair. "RW is more handsome than I remembered. When he's not yelling, or brooding, he has a nice smile."

*Nope, nope, just no.* "You can't still love Dad!"

"I never stopped. The anger and hatred just blocked the good stuff. Time has made me realize that we could be good together. Passionate. Funny."

This was all shades of wrong. "Mother, do you hear yourself? How many years did you tell me how bad things were? How horrible my father was? How you wished you'd never met him."

Claire shrugged. "That was then—this is now. There's a lot at stake here, Chloe. I think we should try again, your father and me. We are older now, more mature. We can make it work."

*What sort of hell is this?*

As Chloe tried to make sense of her mother's words and why she would be saying them, Nicolas came strolling up the path in white shorts. His blue-gray polo shirt made his eyes look amazing. Her gaze took a happy trip over those glorious muscular arms, chest and beautiful legs, and suddenly she couldn't think straight. When he waved at her and gave her a sizzling smile, she could barely breathe.

"Who is that handsome young man?" her mother asked.

*My Nicky M.*

Chloe shook her head and drank her water. He wasn't hers. At least not for longer than this week.

*Do not come in here*, she tried to telegraph to him. Her mother would ruin everything.

He cocked his head, as if studying Chloe's body language through the window. When her mother wasn't looking, Chloe mouthed *sorry* and held up a finger. She tried to convey that she'd be just a minute, but who knew with Mom? It could be an hour that felt like a year.

Frowning, he turned and walked in the other direction.

"Oh, darn. He was easy on the eyes. I was hoping he'd come in and join us," Claire said.

*Over my dead body.* "Um, Mom, I need to get back to work. Are you okay here by yourself?"

"You can't stay for breakfast with your mother? Fine. Go. But ask your father to come down first."

Chloe couldn't fathom how she'd been put in this position. Claire was not good for her father, especially since she'd seen him change after being with Angel.

What was she supposed to do here?

"He's probably busy, Mom."

"When is he not busy? Call him. He'd hang up on me, but he'll listen to you."

Chloe dialed her dad's number, trying to figure out what to say when he picked up.

"Hi, sweetheart. What is it?" Dad answered.

"Um, Mom's here and wondering if you'd like to join her for breakfast."

"No can do. I'm on my way to a business deal."

Surprised that he didn't yell or laugh at the idea, she frowned. "I didn't know you had a meeting today."

There was a long pause.

"I do. An important one. Might be the last I ever have."

What did *that* mean? She hoped it meant he was retiring, but in his current emotional state, she worried Dad might be in trouble. "You haven't been feeling—" she suddenly realized her mother was listening and chose her words carefully "—well. Maybe you should take Jeff with you."

"Not today, Chloe. I've got to do this thing on my own. Which reminds me—I left an envelope for you in my study with a set of keys to the F1. Maybe you should drive Nicolas around, give him a tour of Plunder Cove."

She almost swallowed her tongue. "That's crazy, Dad. You told me to stay away from the F1. If I remember correctly, you said I'd be grounded for life if I went within ten feet of it."

"You were eleven, Chloe. And you'd just crashed your bike into the Lambo. Forgive me for being a little cautious. You're all grown up now. I want you to have it."

Her mouth fell open. "Wait. You're giving it to me?"

"Sure. The color and class remind me of you. It suits you."

Chloe fought the tears since her mother was watching. "That's an amazing gift."

"You are an amazing daughter. Stay sweet. Take care of yourself and your brothers. And tell your mother to go home."

"But what are you doing—?"

The line went dead.

A heavy dose of foreboding settled in her chest.

*What was Dad up to?*

# Ten

Chloe had asked Michele to send a tray of food to Nicolas and to keep him away from the restaurant. Well, away from Claire Harper.

Chloe stayed with her mother as long as she possibly could and then left to go find Nicolas.

He was sitting on a lounge chair by the pool. His long legs were stretched out and he had tucked his left arm behind his head. He looked relaxed and so beautiful that her heart swelled. He had his laptop out and headphones on. Coming up behind him, she could see he was watching a music video. It looked like an audition, which meant he was working on this gorgeous day when she really wanted to *play with him*.

She bit her lip.

No, she meant *show him around Plunder Cove*.

She stepped into his sunlight. "Please tell me you are relaxing and enjoying the day."

*"Senti sua falta, linda."* He moved his glasses down To look at her. "That means 'I missed you, beauty.'" Those gray eyes, that smile, the Portuguese…yep, she couldn't get enough of him.

She pressed her legs together discreetly. "I'm sorry I couldn't join you for breakfast. I was dealing with a crisis." She took a deep breath. "My mother dropped in unexpectedly for my brother's wedding two months ago and never left. But now she's saying she wants to get back together with my dad."

"I could tell it was a tense moment."

"Really? I was trying so hard to scream only on the inside."

He smiled at that. "I read your body."

The ache grew when he left off the word *language*.

"She's gone now. But she'll be back. Hopefully we'll be out of here by then. I'd like to take you on an adventure to introduce you to the area. Is this a good time?"

He closed the laptop. "It's always a good time to have an adventure with you."

"Great." Her voice cracked.

She swallowed hard and reminded herself that her focus was on doing her job today—as a Harper heiress and promoter of the Plunder Cove Resort. She was *absolutely not* going on a date with Nicolas.

Sleeping with him was one thing. But she was not asking for more. At least not during the day.

When the sun went down, she'd see what adventures were in store for her.

He moved the laptop to a drink table and placed the plate of half-eaten food on the table closest to her. Scooting a little, making room on his lounge chair, he opened his arms to her. "Join me. Tell me about this crisis."

No one could see them out here by the private pool. She nestled in under his arm and put her head on his chest. She inhaled. Why did he always have to smell so good?

"Did you have a good relationship with your parents?" she asked.

Nicolas let out a breath. "My father drowned when I was a kid. Fishing accident. My mother never got over it. She suffered from alcoholism, poor nutrition and extreme poverty. It was up to me to take care of her and my four sisters." He'd said the words flatly, as if they didn't sting, but his voice was strained.

She looked up and saw anguish on his face. "Oh, Nicolas. I didn't know."

"My agent kept the bad news out of the media. No one wants to hear why a kid is poor and singing on the street corners, just that he rose up and became famous."

She rubbed his arm, drawing her nails slowly across his skin. "That's why you work so hard."

"I had to. Otherwise my sisters would have starved. They all went to school and are happy and healthy. I'm proud of them. Mom is doing well, too. She got herself dried out and remarried."

She hugged him. "You did so much for your family,

Nicolas. Isn't it your turn to live a little? You don't have to keep working so hard. They are grown and on their own. You should give yourself permission to relax. Take a real, nonworking vacation once in a while."

"Can't. Success is a moving target. If you take your eye off it, even for a moment, it all slips away from you. Besides, I don't know how to vacation. But how did this become about me? Tell me about your mom. You looked like you were the one chewing nails when you were sitting by her. Why?"

"Where to begin? My parents used to fight. A lot. Their words and violence hurt the entire family. It got worse and worse. I could feel the end coming, you know, like a ticking time bomb sitting in the center of the dining room table."

She shuddered and he wrapped his arms around her tighter.

"When the explosion finally happened, my family blew apart. Mom and I were forced out of the house. My brothers were sent away, too. All of us in different directions—shards in the wind. It was terrible. I missed my father and brothers so much. Mom stayed in her room all day, cursing my dad and drinking. I was alone. Broken. No one cared about me. I mostly raised myself." She made a noise of disgust. "Poor little rich girl, right? What you must think of me, complaining about my life when yours was so hard."

He tipped her chin up and melted her with those amazing eyes. "Hey, they're all idiots. You deserved to be a happy kid. So did I, but sometimes life doesn't turn out that way. What you do with the hand you are dealt is the key. Look at how well you turned out."

Chloe didn't usually talk about her painful past. Nicolas was an amazing, sympathetic listener. It was surprising how well they were connecting. Chloe scooped a strawberry off Nicolas's plate and fed it to him. "I used to blame my Mom, but I'm sure my mom was lonely when we were banished from Plunder Cove. She'd never been without a man to support her—first her father and then mine. She went a little bonkers. That's the only reason why a pampered woman who'd never practiced yoga in her life would've read a brochure about a resort in Rishikesh, India, and decided it would be the perfect getaway." She chuckled. "You should've seen her once we got there. She didn't expect that the resort would be rustic, that there would be bugs or poor people or no room service."

He laughed. "Sounds like she read the wrong brochure."

"Or she'd lost her mind. I'm not sure what she sought, but all she found in India was dirt, hunger and a waste of time. In her typical way, Mom demanded her money back."

"Did they return her money?" he asked.

Did he know he was rubbing her arm in slow, sensual circles?

"Most of it. The teachers there don't care about money. They provide tools to assist people on their paths toward spiritual enlightenment. The only thing Mom found in the end was that she hated India. Her fourteen-year-old daughter, on the other hand, found the meaning of life."

He pulled back to look at her. "Really?"

"I was young and my spirit was desperate to be healed. I took to yoga like my first breath. I've always been athletic and flexible, and was able to bend my body into any pose they gave me. They taught me to let go of the past and live in the moment. For the first time in my life, I started to love myself when no one else did. I felt lighter, stronger. Free. India put my feet on a path to happiness."

His smile was warm, genuine. "Maybe you can teach me some of that lighter, free happiness. Unless it requires some sort of twisted pose no one should do."

"No poses. I would love to share what my teachers told me."

He nodded. "I'm a skeptic, but I'll listen."

"Listening is the start. My teachers told me I cannot kill the past, so I might as well make it my friend." She made her voice mimic the old sage she'd loved the most. "Is it not better to sup with an old friend than to have to battle him night after night?"

He laughed. "That's a good imitation."

"I thought it was lousy advice." She shook her head. "I'd rather have wiped out big chunks of my childhood so it would stop hurting. Surely, I thought, there's a meditation or yoga pose for that!"

"Is there?" Nicolas asked. "I'd give that pose a try."

"Apparently not." Now he played with her fingers as she talked. "They taught me to think of the past as grains of sand on the wind—each one forming us, shaping us but not hurting us anymore. The past is gone and the future doesn't exist at all. There is only this moment." She tapped his chest. "And all you have to do during that moment is breathe."

"Just breathe?" Nicolas asked, capturing her hand against his chest. "Is this the advice that drives you to become better?"

"Sounds easy, huh? Maybe for someone dedicated to a spiritual life. For a regular person, it's hard. But the advice reminds me to be present in the here and now."

"Hmm. I guess that's not total mumbo jumbo. As long as it makes you happy."

"I'm working on it. I do think I can help you to be free and happy, too."

He swallowed. "I don't know how to find real happiness, *gata*."

"Neither do I. But what I am trying to do might get us there. Isn't it about time we both try to figure it out?"

They looked at each other for a long moment.

Nicolas finally broke the silence. "What do you want me to say?"

"Say what you feel. That we are worth the effort. That you deserve to be happy."

"It sounds like a lot of effort. But I do want to be happy."

"Good. I think you will like what I have in mind. But first we need to make a pact."

He lifted his eyebrow. "Another deal? If it extends our night, I'm all ears."

"I like your idea of extending our night, but I want to propose another option."

He ran his thumb over her breast. "I'm intrigued. Go on."

She sucked in a breath. It was now or never.

"Remember how you told me that you could prove I am special the way I am?"

He pressed a kiss to her ear, and thrilling waves rolled through her. His deep voice whispered, "My offer was to love you so well that you'd know how special you are."

"I'll accept your challenge if you let me try to prove that you, Nicolas Medeiros, know more about love than you give yourself credit for. I believe you are long-lasting material."

"What?" He flinched.

She rushed on. "I don't mean you have to fall in love with me, or stay with me long-term—I'm not sure *I'm* ready for that. I just think you *could* find yourself loving someone, believing in love. You could have a real, deep relationship…with someone, someday."

He let out a soft breath. "Long-term is not in my makeup, Chloe. I tried. It always ends up a colossal failure. I don't want to hurt you. Or anyone."

"I'm a big girl and I want to do this for you. Give us the week. Let yourself truly feel…free. Enjoy each moment and see where it takes you. Just try."

He closed his eyes. "What if we spend the week together, and at the end it's simply…over. I will go back to LA. What then?"

She kissed his hand. "Then it is what it is. But you and I will have tried. I think it is important for us both to reach for happiness. We might actually find it. What do you think?"

He opened his eyes. She struggled to read the expression swirling in them.

"And all we have to do is…"

"Touch, feel, enjoy each moment together, honestly, fully. Let ourselves be in the present and see what happens. Just breathe. We can find something meaningful for once, together. I know we can."

"I'll get to make love to you whenever I want?" He grinned and pulled her on top of him.

She looked around, made sure her two brothers and father were nowhere in sight. "Mmm-hmm." She kissed him, sinking into his hard body. "As long as there are no Harpers around."

He wrapped his arms around her and kissed the breath out of her lungs. She could feel his heat, waves rolling off his body dancing with hers. She was flying again. She wanted to rip his clothes off right there, in plain sight of any Harper who happened to come swim in the private pool.

He pulled back and studied her face. "You are the most unusual woman I've ever been with. I want you, Chloe. I'll take you any way I can. I'll try to be in the present and breathe and feel—whatever that means. You, *gata*, have a deal." He gripped her butt as he said it.

And sealed the deal by kissing her nipple through her shirt.

# Eleven

When they finally came up for air, Chloe said. "Are you ready for our first work adventure?"

"Every moment is an adventure with you."

She scooted away, feeling weak and giddy. He had a way of stealing all the energy from her cells and electrifying her nerves.

He rose and she got another whiff of his body soap. It made her mouth water. "Let me put my computer in the room, and I will be ready."

"And your cell phone."

A crease formed above those gorgeous eyes. "What?"

"Leave your cell phone, wallet and all your gadgets in the room. I want to untether you from the outside world for a few hours."

"I do not go anywhere without my phone."

She nodded. "I get that. Trust me. It'll be good for you. Those emails, texts and calls will be waiting for you when you get back."

He put his hand on her shoulder. "You'll have to keep me really busy to distract me from the outside world."

She knew she was smiling, but couldn't help herself. "I'll do my best. Let's go," she said.

"Not yet." He spun her around and pressed his lips to hers one more time. Then he tucked a loose strand of hair behind her ear and said, "I don't leave my cell behind."

"I know but—"

He pressed his finger to her lips. "You are making a new man out of me already."

"Meet me in the front. Your adventure awaits." She rose up on her toes, nibbled his chin and then left him to watch her walk away.

Nicolas couldn't stop smiling. He'd made a connection with Chloe, and that didn't come easy with him. She was different and surprising. He had no idea how to live in the present, but he was willing to give the experiment a try for a week. Breathing with Chloe. Hell, as long as they were both naked and he could put his lips all over her soft body, then sign him up. After that? He'd go back to LA. Chloe was amazing but she wasn't going to prove that he was long-lasting material. He wished she could, but he knew it wasn't in him. He'd never be that guy, because he didn't know how to really love anyone other than his family. He never had.

His mind knew all of this. His body, though, seemed

to have a language of its own. When Chloe Harper was near, his fingertips were drawn to her skin, his nose had a heightened awareness of the intoxicating scent of her shampoo and the soap on her body, and his lips longed to taste hers. Loving every inch of Chloe's naked body was a reoccurring theme in his brain.

He waited out front as she'd asked and heard an engine purring in the distance. He sucked in a breath when a volcano-orange McLaren F1 pulled up next to him. It was one of the hottest cars he'd ever seen, especially when the doors bat-winged open to reveal Chloe sitting in the front seat, wearing a white dress and a sexy grin.

"Ready, handsome?" she asked.

*Santa Mãe.* It was going to be a rock-hard day. "This is a McLaren F1 Longtail. Is it even street legal?".

"Yes?" She shrugged. "Probably. I guess so. Most likely."

"Seems legit to me." He climbed in. "You've driven a race car before?"

"Sure. My brothers and I played racing video games all the time when I was a kid. How hard can it be?" She winked at him. "Don't worry. I'll be safe."

The doors closed and he took a long look at the woman in the driver's seat. "It suits you."

She grinned and the look on her face was a mix of excitement and wonder. That suited her, too. If he could get her to look like that in his arms, he would be a happy man.

"That's what he said, too."

He frowned. "Who?"

"My dad when he gave it to me this morning. Let's

take this baby out on the open road and see if you're both right."

She pressed the gas and roared down the drive.

Chloe was giddy. Again.

Taking the curves on an empty backcountry road in her very own race car? Having Nicolas in the passenger seat, eyeing her as if she was a tasty treat? Never in a million years could she have imagined this day. The heck with being professional; she wanted to enjoy the moment. She squealed her delight.

Nicolas laughed. "You are so damned beautiful. A natural-born race car driver. You should get some time on a race track and open her up."

She side-eyed him. "Really?"

He grinned. "It's clear to me, *gata*—you have a need for speed."

She didn't respond. He was correct. Part of her wanted to pull the car over in a lookout spot and grab Nicolas and kiss him like she'd never kissed anyone. Her fingers itched to touch him everywhere.

She added pressure to the gas pedal. The engine purred and she could feel the rumble in her core. She slowed the car and cast Nicolas a glance. "Wow, that felt good."

"You look good." Nicolas's voice was deep, sexy. "Maybe we should pull over. I've never kissed a race car driver before and I want to. Right now."

Excitement raced through her veins. "Mmm. That can be arranged. Let's stop in Pueblicito." Slowly she drove down the main street, while Nicolas took in the small town.

"I've never heard of Pueblicito and yet it looks like it's been here a long time," he said.

"It's probably too small to show up on most maps, but you're right—it has been here since the 1800s. The town started out as a working ranch for my family."

"The pirate Harpers went into ranching?"

"No, the next generations went into cattle and became the land-baron Harpers. It's not a great chapter in my family history." She grimaced. Several chapters in her history were less than stellar. "People have lived in this town all their lives. Several generations back, their descendants were brought here from Mexico to work in the house, fields, pastures or on the range for the Harpers. Those poor people were not always treated well by my ancestors. My father is changing all that." She parked in front of Juanita's Café and Market.

"Your father." He looked puzzled. "RW Harper is upgrading this town, too?"

"In a big way. He is paying the residents of Pueblicito a percentage of all money made on the new resort and restaurant. That is apparently the reason he is going into the resort business to begin with—to give back to the residents in this town and correct past mistakes. Expect to see Pueblicito on the map in a few years."

He cocked his head. "Interesting. It's hard to imagine RW as a charitable guy. I always heard he was a cutthroat businessman. One that shouldn't be trusted."

She laughed. "You aren't wrong. I was skeptical, too. Since I've been home, I am awestruck by how much he has changed from the father I knew growing up. He seems to be making amends and coming through on his promises. It gives me hope that people can change." She opened the doors. "Come on. I can't wait for you to try the dulces here."

They stepped out of the car and were quickly surrounded by a group of young boys ogling her car.

"Aunt Chloe!" her nine-year-old nephew, Henry, came running over. "No way! Grandpa let you drive the F1?"

She smiled and gave Henry a hug. "Even better. He gave it to me."

Henry's face fell. "Is Grandpa okay?"

Henry knew how much RW loved his cars. The kid and his grandpa were remarkably close. The whole family was worried about RW since Angel had disappeared.

"Yep. He's fine." She hoped. "Let me introduce you to my friend. This is—"

"Nicky M!" Julia, Henry's mother, rushed out of the café, letting loose a string of Spanish words as she came. Chloe didn't understand half of it until Julia switched back to a flood of English words. "Holy Madre, I can't believe you're here. I have every record you ever made. Every one. I have watched all your music videos dozens of times. More! Maybe hundreds of times. This is, I mean, I can't even…" She looked at Chloe. "Oh, my gosh, it's Nicky M!"

Chloe laughed. "Yes, I know. Nicolas, this is my sister-in-law, Julia. She's Matt's wife."

*"Con mucho gusto,"* he said in Spanish, not Portuguese, as he shook Julia's hand. "Matt? He is the pilot?"

"Yes."

Chloe elbowed her. "The crowd is growing. Let's go inside."

Julia blinked dreamily and then seemed to mentally shake herself. "Pardon my manners. Of course. Come in. I'll make you two something yummy to eat."

"You're cooking? That's new. Oh, wait." Chloe held up her finger. "Henry?" Chloe called to the boy peeking in the windows of her new car.

Henry held up both hands and took a step back. "I didn't touch it, I swear."

"No, that's fine. If you and your friends are careful, I'll let you sit in my car."

The boys hooted and hollered. "Thanks, Aunt Chloe. We'll be careful," Henry promised.

"Wow. I wish I had an aunt like you when I was a boy," Nicolas whispered as they walked through the glass doors. He put his hand on her back, causing a shiver of delight to roll up her spine.

"I have only one nephew and I reserve the right to spoil him rotten." Chloe inhaled deeply. The sights and smells of the Mexican market never disappointed.

Julia led them to a table in the café. "What would you do with another nephew? Or maybe a niece?"

It was then that Chloe noticed the sparkle in Julia's eye.

"Julia! Really?" Wrapping her arms around her sister-in-law, Chloe gently squeezed. "I am so happy for you. Does Henry know?"

"Not yet. Matt and I are going to spill the beans to-night, after he returns from his flying exercises for the Forestry Service."

"*Parabéns* to you and Matt," Nicolas said. "That is very exciting."

"Nicky M, you could write a song about the excitement in my life. The love of my life returned from the dead, I found my lost mother and now..." The tears welling in her eyes did not dim Julia's radiant smile. "Another baby." She swiped at her wet cheeks. "Stupid hormones."

"Aww. I am so happy for you and Matt. Henry, too. He's going to be a great big brother if he is anything like mine." Chloe kissed Julia's cheek.

"Sit, please. Let me make you lunch," Julia said.

"You've taken over Juanita's while your mom is gone?" Chloe asked.

"Yeah. Has your dad heard from her?" Julia's cheeks were suddenly pale. "I'm so worried."

"Sorry, no." Chloe didn't want to mention the mysterious meeting her dad ran off to this morning. No need to get Julia's hopes up if the meeting had nothing to do with Angel.

Julia sighed. "Let me know if you do, okay? I'm dying to tell her about the new grandbaby. Hopefully that'll convince her to stay here. Now that I finally have a family, I want them all to stay put."

"I get it," Chloe said.

"Family is everything," Nicolas said softly. "I wish my mother would come to California to live, but she refuses to leave Brazil."

"That is rough. I lived most of my life without knowing my mom and dad. It sucked," Julia said.

"Hey, you two should come and hang out with us at the bonfire tonight. Matt invited some of his friends. Jeff and Michele will be there. You could bring your guitar, Chloe. Maybe we can all show Nicky M how talented we are."

"You play the guitar?" Nicolas's eyes were on her.

Chloe could feel her cheeks getting hot. "I try. Just don't ask me to sing, because I don't do that in public."

He leaned into her and lifted his brow. "What would it take to get you to sing for me in private?"

"Um…"

Julia cleared her throat.

"What do you say, Chloe?" Nicolas pulled her into his arms. "Be my date to the bonfire party?"

"Aww. You two make a great couple," Julia said as she walked away to make lunch.

Blood whooshed in Chloe's ears. "But my brothers will be there."

"And?" He laced his fingers with hers. "What are you afraid of?"

She rubbed her thumb on the top of his hand but couldn't look him in the eye. "Messing this whole thing up. With you. With them. Dad. The world." She half chuckled, or at least made a sound that she hoped sounded like a casual laugh. "Yep, that's about it."

"You think if they see us together they'd assume… what? That you are sleeping with me to win the contract?" The tone in his voice! She'd hurt him.

She looked up. "No! Well, maybe. I want them to believe in me. I can't lose my family again."

Tears fell. She couldn't stop them.

"Maybe we can do something else tonight? Just the two of us?"

He leaned forward and looked deeply into her eyes. "I would like to do something else with you before the bonfire party. And after." That grin of his made her wet. "But this is my part of the bargain, proving that you are worthy. And fantastic just the way you are. Look at what you have done already. Not only are you doing your job, convincing me that this place is great for the show, but you are changing me. You've converted a workaholic cell phone addict into someone who can breathe in the present moment and try to become a long-term guy. All in two days! You are a strong force of nature, who I believe can do anything she sets her mind to. If anyone doesn't see how amazing you are, they are the ones messing up. Please say yes and go with me to the bonfire, Chloe. Seize the moment with me."

When he looked at her like that, she would agree to anything. And the thought of before and after was rolling through her brain like a forest fire.

"Nicolas…" she began, her voice thick with need. God, she wanted *before* and *after*. Not to mention tomorrow and next year.

Even though Nicolas was not that guy.

His gaze was on her lips. "Say it, Chloe."

But he was the guy she wanted. Right. Now.

"Yes," she said. "Oh, God, yes."

Nicolas reached across the table, put his hands on

Chloe's wet cheeks and captured her lips. His tongue licked until she opened up and let him set her world on fire. She had never been kissed like that before, especially not at a little table in a small café with people watching. She didn't care about any of her surroundings. Her senses were hypersensitive to him—his touch, sounds, smell, taste. Nicolas was sucking her bottom lip and lighting up every cell in her body.

Life had never felt so good.

*Before* had already begun.

# Twelve

Nicolas had been with a lot of women. He wouldn't apologize for that fact. Some were great lovers, and others helped his career. But most were crutches he leaned on while he limped through his lonely life. And some, like Lila, had tried to destroy him.

Not one of them was like the woman he was kissing in the Mexican café.

Chloe had…something he couldn't quite name. In the music industry he might have called it the It Factor. Still, that seemed shallow when trying to describe the depths of Chloe Harper. What she had went way beyond her brilliant shine, the way she drove a race car, her laughter, the softness of her lips or the wisdom and kindness in her eyes. Whatever it was, it lived within

Chloe, a place he was not good enough to touch or understand. She was simply beautiful.

Far too good for him.

Tonight, he'd go to the bonfire and prove that he was a man who deserved the It Girl.

Julia arrived with a tray full of food. "*Machaca, sopes*, soft tacos, rice and beans."

Chloe pulled her lips away and sat back in her chair. Her cheeks were pink, her braid a little messy and her eyes hooded. Love-drunk was a good look on her.

Nicolas helped distribute the food. "*Obrigado*. Smells good, Julia."

Julia shook her head, giggling. "Nicky M just spoke Portuguese to me. This day keeps getting better."

"I know, right?" Chloe smiled. "That accent is amazing."

Julia left them alone again.

"If I spoke Portuguese to you, would you sing?"

She snorted. "That would be a cruel thing to do to you. But you might convince me to play my guitar…" Her eyes widened. Something over his shoulder caught her attention. "Did you see that man?"

He turned and looked. "Where?"

"Behind the counter. A bald man with tattoos. There. He's staring at you."

"I'm used to people recognizing me. It's one of the hazards of the job. Eat. It's okay. It is nice that you are trying to protect me, but paparazzi is everywhere. Hang around with me long enough and you get used to people staring." For the first time he actually envisioned what it would be like if she was with him in LA.

"I guess I could get used to it. I was worried that the man was spying on us for...well, for another reason." She twisted her napkin between her hands. "I think my dad has kicked a hornet's nest."

He cocked his head. "Meaning?"

She shrugged but fear sparked in her eyes. "My father left today for some secret meeting that he refused to tell me about. On his way out of town, he gave me one of his prized cars. I'm worried about him."

"Why? What is the hornet's nest?"

"Harper business, I guess." She shrugged but he could tell she knew more than she was saying.

"Maybe your father just went for a drive to buy a new F1."

She nodded. "Maybe."

He wanted to ease the tension in her shoulders and make her smile again. "Let's go for a swim."

There it was. The light returned to her eyes and a sexy smile lifted the corners of her lips. "Naked?"

He leaned closer until their noses were almost touching and stroked her leg under the table. "*Mulher*, you read my mind."

"How about we save that for tonight? I have another secret place I'd like to take you to now."

"I'm in your hands."

Julia brought them a bag of candies and reminded them to come to the bonfire. Chloe hugged her and paid, and they left the café. Nicolas wrapped his arm around Chloe as they walked out of Juanita's. His eyes scanned the perimeter, watching for any sign of paparazzi. For the first time in his life, he was the bodyguard protecting the star.

It felt good. He could get used to taking care of a woman like Chloe Harper.

After shooing the little boys away from her car, she and Nicolas climbed in. Putting the pedal to the metal and zooming onto the beach to naked bodysurf was oh, so tempting. Still, she had to slow her revving sex drive the heck down and at least try to salvage the job she was supposed to be doing for her family.

Before she started the car, she said, "There are a few places I'd like you to see."

Leaning over, he moved the dress strap off her shoulder and drew free-form designs on her bare skin with his finger. "I agree wholeheartedly. There are more than a few places I would like to see. Touch. Lick."

Her skin danced in anticipation. She started the car, the rumble adding to her shivers.

Driving down the main street, Chloe gave him the tour of the small town of Pueblicito. "I bet you could film this town as a backdrop for your show. Like you said, it looks old and historical. I envision some of your candidates walking down this street, describing the inspiration for their songs, or maybe talking about their hometowns."

He nodded. "You have a good eye. But I must remind you that it is not a done deal yet. We haven't chosen Plunder Cove as the venue for the show. There are two other locations still to consider."

"I understand."

"I am willing to let you try to convince me, though." She caught the lift of his eyebrow. "More than willing."

His words set off all sorts of warning bells. She pulled the F1 over to the side of the road. "This is what I worry about. If my family thought I threw myself at you just for the contract…" She shook her head. "That's not me. At all. I hope you know that I care about you. I would never sleep with a man for a job or a promotion or…a contract."

"Chloe." He cupped her cheek. "I was joking."

She swallowed hard. "You were?"

"Of course. I've known enough women and men who would sleep with anyone for a career move. You are not one of them."

Satisfied with his answer, she started the car again.

# Thirteen

Chloe drove Nicolas to some of her favorite spots in Plunder Cove, all the while highlighting how the contestants of the show could be filmed in each one. Normally she would take guests to the beach or on one of the boats up the coast, or maybe they'd take out the Jet Skis. Right now, she wanted to do something different with Nicolas, so she took him in the opposite direction—to the mountains.

She parked near the stables. "Let's get out and walk. I don't have the right shoes on, but it's okay. There is a short hike up to one of the most beautiful views in the area, called Lover's Point. Your contestants will love it."

He took her hand in his and they walked up the horse trail and got lost in the Monterey pine forest. When they got to the top, they sat on a large boulder and gazed out across the forest. The green valley below spread like a velvety carpet that ran all the way to the deep blue ocean. A red-tailed hawk cried as it circled overhead. The gentle breeze carried a fragrant mix of pine and sea.

"Wow. I can't even remember the last time I was up here. I forgot how beautiful it was," she said.

"I wish I had my cell phone."

She frowned. It made her sad that he was so connected to his technology that he couldn't enjoy a peaceful moment in nature without his phone. "You probably wouldn't get reception up here anyway."

"No," he captured her chin between his thumb and finger. "I wanted to take a picture of you. This light, the look on your face when you gaze out there… You are beautiful, Chloe."

"Thank you for giving me a chance to be with you, Nicolas. I feel so blessed." She kissed him sweetly, gently pouring all her hope and desire for them into that kiss.

He pulled back and looked at her. Raw amazement lit his features as if he understood the weight of the kiss. The meaning.

"I am awestruck by you," he said.

That melted her through and through. She turned her back on the view and pressed herself into Nicolas. He was caught between a rock and a needy woman. She ran her hands behind his neck while she devoured his lips with kisses that were no longer sweet.

He cupped her butt through the white dress, while his tongue probed her mouth. She was moaning already. His lips pulled away and found the sweet spot on her neck. The electric bolt shot straight through her spine to her toes. Her legs threatened to buckle.

She wanted to feel his skin and quickly began unbuttoning his shirt.

He stilled her hands. "If we keep going like this, I am going to take you here. And it won't be slow. Is that what you want?"

Her head was flying. "Please," she begged. "I need to touch you."

She got his shirt open and ran her fingers over his chest.

He made a guttural groan and ran his hand up her thigh and under her dress. Finding the edge of her panties, he pulled them down. She sucked in a breath and his mouth was instantly on hers. His kisses made her crazy with want, especially with his hand stroking between her legs.

"Chloe," he said in between kisses.

"Hmm?"

"We have a…situation."

That hand was still driving her wild. Fingers dipping in, rubbing, pressing. She tipped her head to the blue sky. "Situation?"

Against her neck, he mumbled. "Someone convinced me to leave my wallet behind. I have no condoms with me."

"Oh." She moved away from his wicked hand and tried to reign in her desire. "Well, we could go back to your room."

"Later. Right now I want to touch you. Make you

feel good. But I can't do it with you looking at me like that. I am too close."

She touched the large bump in his pants. "I could—"

"No. This is for you. Let me do this. Turn around. Hands on the boulder."

She did as she was told. He unzipped her dress slowly, following the zipper down with kisses peppered against her skin. Delight and anticipation rolled through her. Her palms pressed the boulder and she spread her legs a little for balance.

He took her dress off. She was standing on the mountain, wearing only a bra and sandals. A cool breeze blew from the ocean, and the sun warmed her shoulders. Her body was a live wire of anticipation. She waited to see what Nicolas was going to do next.

"Don't move," he said.

One of his warm hands were on her hip. She heard him rustling behind her. Squatting?

He kissed the back of her knee and she jerked.

"You moved," he said. "I'm in a precarious spot. I don't want to fall down the hill today."

"Sorry." She pressed herself harder into the boulder.

He kissed her there again and she didn't knock him off the mountain. "Better." He kissed her inner thigh and she twitched. She was hypersensitive and loving it.

"God, Nicolas. Your kisses are electrifying me."

"Is that a good thing?"

"So good. More, please."

He kissed her bare bottom and she was suddenly panting. He rose, standing behind her. She could feel his pants against her bare legs. Moving her braid away, he nibbled on her shoulder blade, making his way to her neck. One hand wrapped around her belly, holding her to him. The other…

"Oh, yes," she moaned when his hand cupped her. One finger dipped inside her—moving in and out—while his palm exquisitely pressed her nub.

He nibbled on her neck and his fingers did magical, wonderful things inside her. "Come for me, baby."

She let go. The waves rolled over and over her, higher and higher, as if they'd never end.

"*Minha paixão*, you are gorgeous," he said into her ear.

*Minha paixão?* She'd look up that expression later. As she started to come down, one warning bell rang out through her love-hazed brain. *I'm in trouble here.*

Her eyes were shut. She could feel his breath on her skin, hear his deep voice rolling through her, smell his manly, delicious scent, feel her body floating with pleasure. She was fully present.

Fully, wholly…his.

She sensed he was trying to go with the flow, but he wasn't there yet. And at the end of the week, he would be going back to LA. What was she going to do about that?

"Wow." She put her dress back on. "I've never experienced anything like that."

She wrapped her arms around him and petted his bare chest. Memorizing his warm skin and muscles as her fingers stroked every inch. She kissed his chest, collarbones and that dip between his pecs.

He wrapped his arms around her and kissed the top of her head. Neither one of them spoke.

She held him like that for several long moments and pretended that he would always be hers.

Something had happened between them on the mountain.

Nicolas felt it with blinding intensity. It started with that sweet, gentle kiss. He had never been kissed quite like that before. And then when she came for him with such wild trust…*wow* was the word.

Nicolas felt closer to Chloe than he had felt to any woman in years. Maybe in his whole life.

What was it about Chloe Harper?

"I have to work today," he said softly. "Just a few hours." He also needed a cold shower and a few moments alone to figure things out. It was all new to him.

She was getting to him in ways he had never experienced. It was exhilarating and worrisome all at once. He was usually in better charge of his emotions and the situation. When he was with Chloe, control was far from his reach.

He'd held her on the top of that mountain and realized that he truly wanted the pure, deep, all-in type of relationship that she was offering.

But something whispered from the broken hole inside his being, *You will screw it up, Nicolas. You always do.*

And it would hurt worse than what Lila had done to him. He knew this instinctually because he hadn't given all of himself to Lila. He'd always held something back. For Chloe, he'd have to give everything.

*Was he capable of such a sacrifice?*

He honestly didn't know the answer, but he sure as hell better figure it out before he dove any deeper with the woman in his arms.

"Perhaps we should head down now," he said.

"Of course."

She pulled back and the breeze chilled his skin through his open shirt. He would be lying if he said he wasn't a little disappointed when she left his arms.

As they walked back down the hill to the car, she talked almost nonstop about different scenes she could picture in the show. It was nervous chatter, as if he'd knocked her off her feet, too. He wasn't the only one with emotions soaring over the mountain.

And then she surprised him again by dangling the car keys in front of his face.

"Want to drive?" she asked.

"You'll let me drive your race car down the mountain?"

She nodded. She trusted him.

He whooped, scooped her up in his arms and swung her around in a circle. *"Cada momento que passa eu me apaixono mais por você."*

Laughing, she said, "Is that a yes?"

Chloe had dropped Nicolas off at the front of the mansion and circled back to park the car in the garage. Very, very carefully she pulled in next to the Ferrari and cut the engine. She was alone in her car when she pulled out her cell phone and translated as best as she could what Nicolas had said to her in Portuguese.

*With each passing moment, I fall more for you.*

She pressed her hand to her heart. Did he mean it? She hoped he did and yet it scared her because she was falling fast for him. Too fast. She knew she should enjoy every moment, should feel it all, savor her time with Nicolas and not think about the future.

She wished she could answer the burning question: *If I truly embrace the moment, how can I protect my heart from the hurt at the end?*

Chloe wasn't a teenager anymore. Or a fool. She knew Nicolas's track record with women; heck, she knew her own lousy record. The odds weren't in their favor to have a loving and successful relationship.

But she wanted to try.

"We deserve to be happy," she said to the universe. "Please give us a break."

Determined to fight for what she wanted, she went into the house. First, she checked in on her father. He hadn't returned yet and none of the workers in the house knew where he was. She was still worried about him, but she knew he could handle himself. And he'd ask for help if he needed it. He'd changed so much.

Passing by Nicolas's room, she put her hand on his door for just a moment, but did not disturb him. Music played inside, which probably meant he was working. It was a good time to stretch some of the angst out of her muscles before the bonfire party.

She put on her yoga pants and T-shirt, and took her mat outside.

# Fourteen

Nicolas was having a tough time focusing on music videos. He'd had to play the last one three times because his mind kept wandering back to a particular blonde *gatinha* and her "kiss me" lips. It was suddenly too warm in his room to work or even think straight. He put on a pair of shorts and went out to the patio in the hopes of catching a breeze. What he caught instead was an eyeful. His girl was sexy stretching again.

To hell with work. He slipped on his running shoes and went out to join her.

Her sweet backside was high in the air when he approached, and it was all he could do not to put his hand on her firm glutes.

He leaned against a tree, crossed his arms and said, "Don't mind me. I love to watch you do that."

"Why just watch?" She broke his heart by dropping to her knees and effectively moving her sweet *bunda* from his reach. "I can show you some yoga moves." She stretched up, opening her chest, arching her back. "Are you finished with your work for today?"

He was now. She was so damned sexy.

"What do I need to do?"

When he sat on her mat, she put her hands on his shoulders and massaged. "Relax. Be open to the experience, let lightness fill your chakras."

He shook his head. "I have no idea what that is, but I am open to the experience of you touching me." And he liked the pretty pink flush that was spreading across her chest.

She had him sit cross-legged. "Close your eyes. Breathe lightness all the way to the bottom of your belly. Hold it. Release all the pain from your past in a deep exhale. Slowly. Good. Breathe in light, let out fears." Over and over he did as she told him. With his eyes still closed, she massaged his jaw, starting at his ear all the way down to his chin—slow, sensual pressure.

"I am releasing the stress in your jaw. Keep breathing," she said.

"It feels good," he said. He wanted that pressure all over his body.

When she was done with his jaw, she placed a light kiss on his lips. "Okay, now we practice yoga. First stretch up. Inhale, filling your lungs." She lifted her arms and chest high. "And exhale while swan diving toward the mat and let yourself hang in a forward fold."

He did as he was told three times. "Piece of cake."

"Yeah, you've got this. Okay, the next pose is called Downward Dog. Let me show you how to do it."

She pressed her hands and bare feet into the grass next to the mat, and her cute ass was pointed toward him. It was his favorite pose. *Muito gostosa.*

"You try," she said.

He did his best but was sure his pose didn't look sexy.

"Close. But…" She stood up. "Mind if I put my hands on your, um…?"

He grinned. "Please. Touch my *um* all you want."

She coughed. "*Hips.* That's what I meant to say."

Coming up behind him, she wrapped her hands around his hip bones and gave them a gentle tug. "Pull your hips back to right about here. Tailbone toward the sky."

Her words were businesslike, but that husky tone was driving him wild. He wished he could see her face instead of staring down at the mat. Her hands held him in place, and his tailbone wasn't the only body part reaching for the sky. If only she would bring her hands forward a bit.

"Perfect." She released him and the coldness rushed in. It happened every time she removed her hands from his skin. Getting down beside him, she did the dog pose, too.

"Now we are going to lower ourselves down to a plank position. Sort of like the start of a push-up. Just hold it," she said. "Good. That's it, except lower your butt a little."

He did. "Like this?"

"Too much. I'll show you." She stood up and straddled him. And then she put both hands on his glutes. Only she didn't just lower his body to the correct position. She rubbed his butt for a long beat, as if enjoying the bunching of his muscles under his cotton shorts.

Why did his friend Tony say he hated yoga?

"This dog likes that," he said.

"Oh! I'm… That's not… I didn't mean to…" Surprise made her voice rise, and the warmth from her hand was gone. Still in a plank position with her straddling him, he felt her moving away before he saw her go.

"Wait," he growled.

He turned over, reached up, grabbed her wrist and pulled her on top of him. Her body on his was perfect. He kissed her like the hungry dog he was.

Her hands gripped his shoulders. She kissed him back, just as greedily. Her legs were on top of his, and her breasts were against his chest. He could feel the pounding of her heartbeat. And the blessed heat between her legs. Her braid dangled by his face. He wrapped the braid around his hand and gave it a gentle tug, exposing her neck.

"I like this pose the best," he whispered against her neck. He cupped her butt with the other hand and pressed her down harder against his aching erection.

She moaned and ground herself against him.

He was close to coming already, if she made that sound again or moved, even a little, it would be difficult to stop himself. Normally he had better control, but with Chloe control went out the window.

Releasing her braid, he ran his hands up her shirt, going on a relentless search to touch as much soft skin as possible. He unhooked her bra from the back and continued forward until he had one of her breasts in hand.

She inhaled. Her eyes wide. "We shouldn't…"

But she didn't get up, didn't release his shoulders. He watched her swallow. Her eyes locked on to his. It seemed like a storm was brewing inside her deep blue irises. The golden feathers were taking flight.

What was she thinking?

"Not here," she said. Her pink tongue swiped across her bottom lip. "Your room or mine?"

"Wherever you want me."

"Everywhere. When I'm with you, touching you, I want more. Crave more. You are all I think about. Please take me to your room and…." She bit her lip. "I want to make you feel good like you did for me."

He ran his hand over her breast. "The licking? Kissing? Sucking?"

"Oh, God, yes." She rolled off him and his body felt bereft.

He stood up, feeling lighter than he had in years. Was that his chakras he was feeling or desire? Didn't know. Barely cared. All he could think about was Chloe.

"Leave the mat," she said. "And hurry."

# Fifteen

RW sat in an unmarked car, outside the house where he hoped to save the woman he loved.

The man who had been chasing Angel all these years was inside. RW felt alive and filled up with white-hot... redemption. He would keep Cuchillo away from Angel once and for all.

The plan he'd begun with Angel's help was working. Matt and Jeff were finally happy with women who loved them. With Nicolas in Plunder Cove, Chloe was going to be happy, too. His children had each other; the people of Pueblicito had the resort.

Saving Angel by ending Cuchillo would be RW's last great act.

"Is the wire working?" RW asked, pressing it to his chest to make sure it was still there.

The detective who'd helped RW get to this point checked the system. "Yeah, don't touch it. We're good to go."

RW opened the car door and stepped out. Quietly he walked across the street and toward the house. But as a car approached, RW stepped behind a tall juniper bush.

The car door opened and a woman stepped out. She stood for a long moment, staring at the gate and waiting for…what? She looked around nervously, as if sensing that she was being watched. And when her face turned toward the juniper bush, RW's heart nearly fell out of his chest. Even though it was dark as he peeked through the bushes, he was sure. He'd recognize her beautiful face anywhere.

*Angel.*

He was so stunned that he didn't move. He didn't yell. His brain was exploding with questions, the foremost being—what in the hell was she doing here?

Squaring her shoulders, she quickly walked toward the gate. She was going in.

*No, damn it, no.*

RW rushed out of the bushes, toward Angel. He had to stop her before Cuchillo saw her. He'd throw his body over hers, promise Cuchillo the world, anything to protect her. Before he could get to her, the door opened.

Angel went inside. Willingly.

RW moved close to an open window. He needed to plan carefully. He couldn't see, only hear. His heart was pounding in his ears.

"I never thought I'd see you again, *Ladronita*," a man's voice said. "Missed me? Search her."

"She's clean, Cuchillo," a woman said.

"Smart girl. Why are you here?" Cuchillo asked.

"To ask you to stop chasing after me. No more threats. Don't kill anyone else because of me."

"Kill anyone? You've been watching too much television, *mujer*. We are a good group of people. You know that."

She laughed. It wasn't the joyful sound RW enjoyed hearing. This was a sound of disgust. "I am not wearing a wire, Cuchillo. There have never been lies between us. Why start now?"

"No lies, then. You know what I am going to say."

More silence. RW could imagine the dipping of her head in acknowledgment. She did know. She'd told RW what Cuchillo would say and do if he ever caught up with her. That dire promise had been why RW had plotted and planned to get to this point.

"I plucked you off the street and brought you into the family, into my home. You became an extremely skilled thief, *Ladronita*, truly brilliant. And yet I never would've believed you could steal from me. You robbed me of the only things I care about. Family. Legacy. You don't steal those things, *mujer*. Give them back."

"I can't do that, Cuchillo," she said.

There was silence in the room. RW held his breath as he thought of the family Cuchillo referenced—Matt's wife, Julia. Angel's daughter. The one she'd fled with and hid to protect. Angel had sacrificed so much for Julia, for RW.

He would do the same for her, even if it meant fighting his way in to give her a chance to escape.

"You stole *from me*!" Cuchillo roared. "My own flesh and blood. My only child. Bring me my little girl."

"She is a grown woman who makes her own decisions," Angel said in a voice that was surprisingly calm. RW admired her courage so damned much. "I could ask her if she wants to meet you. At a public place of our choosing, hers and mine. You will stop looking for us after that."

"Interesting proposition. I will agree to let her go, if she chooses." Cuchillo went on, "But you, *Ladronita*? You are another *cosita linda*. You must pay for your crimes against me. Against our family."

RW searched the bushes for a rock or heavy stick. Quietly he crept along the building.

"I never talked. You know that," Angel said.

Cuchillo growled, "You did talk because old-man Harper knows. His private eye talked, *mujer*. People always do."

There on the ground, RW found what he was looking for. Not a rock, but a hammer. RW picked it up.

"Please, Cuchillo, let it go. RW doesn't know much, I swear," she said.

*I know enough.*

"Get ready, Cuchillo," RW whispered, readying the hammer.

"To pay off your crimes, you go back to your rich old man and give me something of his—equal value plus ten years' of interest—and I will let you go."

"Steal from RW?" Angel's voice cracked. "I can't. I won't."

"Fine. Then you pay, here and now. And I'll find my baby girl without you."

"No!" her voice exploded through the room. "Don't try to contact her, Cuchillo. Leave her alone."

"I will do what I want. She is my flesh and blood," he barked.

When Angel cried out in pain, RW saw red and moved toward the door.

"Okay. I'll do it," Angel whimpered.

*Wait.* RW stopped. *She's going to do what?*

"I'll… I'll steal from RW. Just let me talk to my daughter first. Give her a chance to make up her own mind and meet you on her own terms. It'll be better for her…and for you."

"Fine. We have a deal. Do not break it, *mujer.*"

RW lowered the hammer and backed away into the shadows. Why had she gone back to Cuchillo? Why didn't she trust that RW could protect her?

Angel, his beautiful Angel, the woman he was willing to risk his life for was finally coming home.

To rob him.

# Sixteen

Chloe was in Nicolas's room. Both of them were in Nicolas's favorite state—naked.

"Oh, my." She smiled at all the manly beauty before her. *"Quão lindo."*

"It turns me on when you speak Portuguese." He crawled on top of her. His dreamy blue eyes locked with hers. "More, please."

She ran her hands through his hair. *"Obrigado. Cachaça. Rio de Janeiro."*

"Ay, *gata*. What you do to me. You must learn this one." His lips hovered over hers. *"Me beije."*

"What does it mean?"

"Kiss me."

*"Me beije,"* she said softly.

His lips were on hers and his gaze never wavered. Her heart raced and yet everything else slowed down.

"But it's my turn to make you feel good." She pushed him over on his bed and had her way with him. It was her desire to kiss him from toe to head, but she got distracted by his glorious midsection and lingered until he cried out.

Feeling powerful and complete, she kissed his belly.

"Come up here." He took her by her arms and pulled her to him. His expression resembled awe. How could that be? He'd been with many beautiful women in his life. She was no supermodel. No actress. No famous singer. She was simply Chloe Harper.

He kissed her slowly, deeply. She saw so much emotion on his handsome face. She'd had fantastic sex in her life and had been with a few handsome, sexy men, but never, never had she been kissed like this. Until Nicolas. He kissed her like she was a goddess. It brought tears to her eyes.

One of his hands went around her waist and roamed over her back, caressing, pressing, loving. He gripped her butt and pressed her to him.

*"Minha linda."*

She understood that phrase. *My beauty.* Still didn't quite believe the words, but liked hearing them. She clung to him, naked, with both arms and legs around him, and pretended that she was his. For now. This was the best moment of her life and it might not last.

Tears burned hot in her eyes again. She didn't dare voice her fears.

*Oh, my God, this is what love feels like? Why does it hurt so much?*

"Are you okay?"

"Sorry I'm so emotional. I'm loving this."

He grinned. "Me, too. I'm ready." He slipped on the condom and entered her.

"Yes. Deeper," she said.

He obliged and went in deeper, harder, thrust after thrust. It was driving her wild. She bucked under him, taking him in, matching his speed, giving back in turn. It was no slow, deliberate dance, but more of a frenzied pounding of drums in the midst of a firestorm. Could a desperate woman burn up from so much heat? And still she needed more. Deeper. Faster.

They moved together—one breath, one heart, a driving insatiable thirst for release. She was close, so close. Gripping him with everything she had, she held on, wanting it all to last.

She felt him start to shudder and let herself go. She joined him as they shot up and over the sun. He collapsed on top on her.

Emotions, so powerful that she couldn't sort them out, rolled over her. Tears wet her cheeks.

"Chloe?" He sat up. "Did I hurt you?"

*Yes. No.* Her heart had shattered, for she knew, really knew that she had fallen hard for him. She wanted to keep him.

Forever.

"I'm fine," she lied and rushed to get up and hide in the bathroom until her tears stopped and she could get control of herself.

"Wait." He jumped up off the bed and stood before her in all his naked glory. "Tell me. What's wrong?"

"Nothing. That's just it." She lifted her chin and looked him in the eyes. "You are insanely perfect. It's me. I want too much and am afraid I can't have what I need."

"What does that mean?"

She chewed her lip. The tears threatening to rain down and ruin everything. "I don't want it to end, Nicolas."

He gave her a smoldering look and ran his finger down her chest. "Who says it has to end? I was just getting started."

"But it will end. You're going back to LA."

There was something there—in his eyes, the turn of his lips—that she wished she hadn't seen. She'd wounded him.

"Don't give up on me, Chloe." His voice was choked with emotion, too. "I'm working on giving you...us... what we both need."

She swallowed but the lump in her throat wouldn't budge. He shook his head. "Am I doing this wrong, sweetheart? Tell me what you want."

The tears came. "You, Nicolas. I want you. I always have."

"So take me, Chloe." He wrapped his arms around her. "I'm here."

She ran her hands around his neck and kissed him, pouring all her mixed-up emotions into that kiss. Taking his comfort. His passion. Needing so much to believe this was real.

He pulled her back to the bed and she kissed him just like she wanted. Soft, deep, real.

And he flipped her over on her back. "Now I'm taking what I want."

The kissing and licking started at her jawline. When he got to her chin, he nibbled. "Mmm, honey."

She laughed. The tears were gone. "I don't taste like honey."

"You are right. You taste better." He kissed her neck, and waves of desire rolled through her.

*Oh, wow. How did he do that?*

He dipped his tongue in her ear and she almost lost her mind. He sucked her earlobe and whispered, "You know what I want?"

*To torture me with desire?* "What?"

"To make you come again. At least two more times."

She sucked in a breath, her heart thundering in her chest. "Is that so?"

"Just relax."

Hard to do when he was kissing her breasts again.

"I am going to take my time here. Go real slow." His tongue circled her erect nipple.

"You don't have to go too slow."

"My turn to call the shots, *gata*. I've got a lot of licking and sucking to do. And a whole lot of honey to dip my tongue into." He lifted his eyebrow and burned her with his sexy grin. "I do this thing. I've been thinking about showing you how it feels all day. Can I show you now?"

*Holy moly.* "You do a thing? With your tongue?"

"Lie back and see."

She lay back and quickly learned that Nicolas had a wicked, wicked tongue. She closed her eyes and let the man of her dreams kiss her worries away.

# Seventeen

Chloe asked Robert, her dad's driver, to drop her and Nicolas off at the beach. She had her guitar and a beach blanket for them to sit on.

"Can I carry that?" Nicolas pointed to the guitar.

"Sure. Thanks."

It gave her a happy little zing when he linked his fingers with her free hand as they walked toward the bonfire. He gave her hand a reassuring squeeze. She side-eyed him to make sure he was comfortable with the idea of hanging out with her family tonight. He seemed fine—jaw relaxed, shoulders not climbing up to his earlobes, a soft smile lifted his lips. She probably looked the same. It had been a long time since she had felt so good. He'd loved all the stress out of her limbs.

"Aunt Chloe! You're late." Henry ran toward them. "We're making s'mores."

"Yum." She smiled at her nephew. "My favorite."

"Hey, Fish made it," Matt called out.

"Fish?" Nicolas asked.

"It's my nickname. I used to spend hours and hours in the ocean, chasing after these two—bodysurfing, swimming to the buoys and doing handstands in the water." She leaned closer and whispered. "We'll swim later."

"Finally," Jeff said, to which Michele playfully slapped his arm.

Chloe blushed. "Yeah, uh, sorry we're late."

Matt was watching her with a strange look on his face. Concern? "You missed my friends from my Forestry volunteer work. They had to go. We still have some of the tri-tip and I think there are some Santa Maria beans left, but the rest is gone."

"They all ate like it was their last meal," Julia said.

"I tried to get them to wait, but…" Jeff raised both hands.

Did Jeff give her a weird look, too? They were both worried about her. Protective. Huh. She did not expect that. At least their expressions didn't seem to be judgmental. Maybe Nicolas had been right all along when he thought her brothers wouldn't judge her for having a boyfriend. Her heart squeezed.

*Boyfriend?* Was that what Nicolas was?

In an attempt to not look any of her family members in the eyes while she sorted out all the crazy thoughts in her head, she spread the blanket down on the sand. The blush was already warming her neck and cheeks.

"My fault," Nicolas said. "Chloe was showing me her yoga moves."

"I bet she was," Michele mumbled.

Julia fake-coughed.

Could they all tell she'd been having wicked sex with the man of her dreams?

"Henry, how about you make me a s'more?" Chloe changed the direction of the conversation. "Nice and toasty."

"Sure thing, Aunt Chloe!" Little Henry hustled off to stake a marshmallow for her.

"You brought your guitar. Are you going to sing for us, sis?" Matt elbowed her.

She snorted. "Right. Nicolas doesn't want his ears to bleed."

"Come on, you're good. You used to sing a lot," Matt said.

"Yeah, all the time. Day and night, everywhere. Seriously annoying, but I liked your voice," Jeff said.

What were her brothers trying to do to her? She stopped singing long ago because her Dad told her to stop the noise when she was small. She had craved love and needed attention and had been devastated when her dad had shut her up. Her heart had broken and her voice went silent. She never sang in public again. And she for sure would not sing in front of Nicolas now. "Uh-uh. You two are nuts. Maybe Nicolas will channel his younger self and treat us with a song, though. I can strum along, or he can use my guitar."

Nicolas rubbed her shoulder. "I would like to hear you sing. No judgments."

As much as she loved him rubbing her skin… "My brothers are joking around. Ignore them. Let's eat. I'm starved."

They all got comfortable around the campfire. Michele sat in front of Jeff on a blanket, leaning against him. He played with her hair. Julia sat behind Matt, rubbing his neck and shoulders, while their son squatted next to them in marshmallow-roasting bliss. It was the picture of a happy extended family. Chloe's heart melted. She'd wanted to be a part of this scene for so long that she'd almost given up hope that it would ever happen. And yet here she was. It made her happy that her brothers had both found true love.

"Shall we?" She motioned for Nicolas to sit down on the blanket she'd brought. She sat beside him. Shoulder to shoulder. Touching but not nearly enough in her book. His body heat was lifting the hairs of her arm, and his manly fragrance was making her achy again.

Gosh, she was always in a state of want around this man.

She had to focus on something other than her insane desire to push him back on the blanket and have her way with him. "Hungry?" she asked.

"Starved." He gave her a lazy, sexy glance. "For something as sweet as honey."

She swallowed loudly, remembering how he'd tasted her as if she was the best dessert he'd ever had. Bumping him with her elbow, she whispered. "Later."

"Promise?"

She nodded. Her imagination was already getting ahead of her.

He took her hand and said far too loudly. "Okay, then. I'm going to hold you to me."

Everyone stopped talking. All eyes were on her.

"The expression is *hold you to it*," Jeff corrected him.

Nicolas lifted his shoulders casually and looked her in the eye. "Not the way I do it."

Chloe sputtered. "Tri-tip! Can we eat now, Matt?"

They ate their share of barbecue meat and beans, and had their fill of s'mores while Matt shared some of the search and rescue stories that he'd assisted on with the Forestry team. Matt didn't need to work because he was the heir to the Harper family fortune but he volunteered as a pilot for the forestry service because her loved rescuing people who were in trouble or lost. He'd always loved flying. His little boy hung on every word, but Chloe could see that his eyes were getting heavier and heavier. It was late for him. Finally, Henry curled up next to his mom and fell asleep.

When the conversation hit a lull, Nicolas picked up the guitar.

Her teenage, fan-girl self silently squealed. Her mature self politely clapped to cheer on her man and then promptly had heart palpitations. Was he really her man? It was crazy and so sweet at the same time. But mostly crazy. Her emotions were a hot mess.

"Are you going to sing 'Baby, Come After Me'?" Michele asked.

"And are you going to dance?" Julia pressed her hands to her heart. "I used to love watching you dance."

"Hey, I thought you loved watching me dance," Matt grumbled.

"I do, *amor*. But Nicky M was…" Julia fanned herself and didn't finish the sentence.

Everyone chuckled. Chloe knew exactly what Julia meant, but suddenly didn't want him dancing for anyone but her. She truly had lost her mind. "No, we will not make him dance."

"I'd dance with you," he said to her.

"How about Saturday night at the restaurant opening?" Michele said. "We'll have a small orchestra and you all can show off your moves. Maybe my hubby will spin me around the floor."

"Jeff?" Chloe laughed. "I hope you have steel-toed shoes."

"Hey! I'm not a ballroom champ like Matt, but I'm not a bad dancer," Jeff complained. To Michele, he said, "I'll spin you like you've never been spun."

"Promises, promises." Michele winked at Chloe. They had a running joke that Jeff would make any excuse not to dance. He wasn't bad; he was just such a perfectionist that he hated that he wasn't great at it. Apparently, a little healthy competition was going to get him out there.

Nicolas had a wistful look on his face as he watched the family discussions. Did he miss his own family? She rubbed his arm.

"Nicolas, as much as I loved your big hit, my favorite song was that soft one. What was it called? 'Meu Doce Amor'?" Michele asked. "Will you play that one?"

*My Sweet Love.* Chloe sighed. "I love that one, too. I learned to play the guitar to that song."

"Yeah, no duh. She strummed that song a million times until I heard it in my sleep. My sister taught herself." There was a fierce pride in Jeff's tone. "She's amazing like that."

"Stubborn and determined. It runs in the Harper blood," Matt added.

"No duh," Julia laughed.

"From now on, when I sing it, I will think of you," Nicolas said to Chloe.

She pressed her hand to her chest like Julia had done earlier. "That's the nicest thing anyone has ever said to me."

"Come." He motioned for her to sit in front of him. "You play. I'll sing."

She sat cross-legged and picked up the guitar. She could not lie—the thought of playing the song in front of Nicolas made her hands tremble. Casually, as if it was the most natural thing in the world, he put one hand on her thigh. The zing shot through her body.

"Relax. Breathe in light, let out fears," he whispered in her ear. "You've got this."

Repeating her yoga mantra back to her word for word? Could he be any more perfect? She smiled at him. "Piece of cake."

She strummed and he sang the melody next to her. To her. His voice was deeper than it used to be, richer, sexier. She didn't need to focus on the chords, for her fingers knew how to play this one by heart. Instead she turned to watch him.

The way he looked at her when he sang…

His gaze was sizzling hot—as if he meant the words. The lyrics about everlasting love and forever promises caressed her skin like soft rose petals. For years she had wanted to believe that this song he wrote was nothing but pure truth. That it was possible for her to fall in love with someone who wouldn't send her away. But the truth she knew up until today proved the song to be nothing but a fairy tale. She had stopped playing it a long time ago because it broke her heart. No one loved her like the lyrics promised. There wasn't a person in her life who hadn't abandoned her.

When Nicolas got to the last line, he sang it softly and straight to her. "My love, my sweet love, forever mine."

She stopped playing. The tears welled in her eyes. For a long beat they stared at each other in silence, as if they were the only two people on the beach, next to a crackling fire.

And then her family clapped.

"You were great." His voice was thick with emotion. "I have performed that song many times, but never like that. What you do to me, *gata*." He wiped the tear off her cheek with his thumb. "Come." He stood and offered his hand to her. Sexy desire hooded his eyes. To the others, he said, "Thank you for a nice evening."

She blinked and let him pull her to her feet. "We're leaving?"

His thumb made slow circles on the palm of her hand. "*After* is about to begin."

"Wait!" Jeff rose to his feet, too. "I need to speak to you, Nicolas."

"Now?" Chloe asked.

"Yes, now. I'll take Nicolas back to his room and Matt, you bring Chloe back."

Nicolas's eyes narrowed.

"What is this about, Jeff?" Chloe asked.

Matt rose, too. "I need to talk to you about something important, Fish. Sorry, man." He shook hands with Nicolas. "Family matters."

*Dad.* Her heart pounded. Why didn't they say so earlier? Was that why her brothers had looked so worried?

"I understand. See you later, Chloe." Nicolas placed a gentle kiss on her cheek.

"You better. I can't wait for after."

When Jeff's car pulled out of the lot, she turned to Matt and her sisters-in-law. "Spill it. What's going on?"

"It's your father, Chloe," Michele said.

"I think it has something to do with my mom, too," Julia added.

"My sources say he's been talking to the FBI to try to help Angel, to stop that gang she used to be involved in. Stupid. He should stay out of it."

"He loves her, Matt," Chloe said. "He'll do what he has to do to save her."

"He's not in the right frame of mind and shouldn't be driving himself anywhere."

"Driving himself?" Chloe asked. RW Harper didn't

put his hands on a steering wheel. He had drivers for that.

"The Bugatti is not in the garage. No one has any clue where he went. Dad's gone missing."

# Eighteen

Nicolas rode back to Casa Larga from the bonfire with a very quiet Jeffrey Harper. Chloe had taught him to notice body language, and her brother had the telltale signs of tension. Something was on the man's mind.

Harper parked the car in front and turned off the engine. "Chloe is a very special lady."

No question there. "Yes, she is."

"No, I don't think you understand. She is important, beautiful, fragile. Chloe means the world to me and I will do everything to protect her."

Nicolas crossed his arms. This aggressive-brother act was nothing new. He'd had to deal with posturing before. It came with the territory of dating lots of women.

"Duly noted."

Jeff shook his head. "I know your type. Hell, I was

your type. You can date anyone you want. Women drop from the sky, right into your lap."

Nicolas laughed. "Not exactly."

"But it's easy for you to make a woman's head spin. Especially Chloe's. She has been in love with you for most of her life."

Nicolas swallowed hard. Being a fan was not the same as love.

"She had it rough, man. Really rough." Jeff went on. "Some people should never have kids, and our parents were the worst. Chloe was always so eager to please, so sensitive. She loves people deeply and gives her whole heart away even when she gets nothing in return. She took care of me when I needed her. She'd stand outside my door and belt out her silly little songs. Until my dad shut her up." Jeff cussed under his breath. "Bastard ruined her, broke her free spirit. Matt and I protected her as much as we could, but then we were sent away and Chloe was left behind with that nasty woman we call *Mother*. It's a wonder she survived."

"*Droga*. She said her childhood was hard. I didn't understand how bad it was."

"I'm telling you this so you don't mess it up, Medeiros. Chloe means more to me than your business. More than the restaurant or my reputation. She's more family to me than my parents ever were."

"I understand."

"Again, I don't think you do. She cares for you—I can see that—probably too much already. It's not you— it's her. Part of her has been starving for love and attention her whole life and yet she has nothing to show

for it. She'll pour her soul and heart into making this…
*thing* between you into a real relationship because that's
what she desperately wants. She deserves to have a man
who will love her and cherish her for keeps."

Nicolas swallowed hard. The question was, did he
deserve her?

"Let's cut to the chase." Jeff leaned in close. "Chloe
is all that matters. Hurt her, and my brother and I will
destroy you."

"I don't want to hurt her," Nicolas growled.

"But you will, right? It's what you do."

Nicolas didn't answer. They both knew the truth.

"Walk away now, Medeiros. I'll tell her you had an
emergency back in Los Angeles and had to go. Matt
will fly you back tonight."

Nicolas got out of the car but he didn't walk away
yet. He leaned through the window and said, "No matter what happens, you need to do better by your sister.
All you Harpers do."

Jeff frowned. "Me? What did I do?"

"You let her believe that she is not worthy of this
job, of your love, of being a Harper—all of it. You better square that with her, or you will be hearing from
me." Sure, he was growling, but he had the right. The
Harpers had hurt Chloe and should feel pain for that.

Jeff's eyes widened. "She thinks that? Hell, Medeiros, she's the best of all of us."

"Then tell her, Harper. Prove it to her. Make her
understand one-hundred-and-fifty percent that she is
wanted here."

Jeff shook his head. "She is wanted. She's my family."

"I'm not the one you need to convince."

"All right. I'll make sure she knows how important she is to me, to our family. Your conscience is clear. But can you promise me that you are the best man for my sister?"

He breathed in and then out. It didn't help. He was still Nicolas Medeiros. "No. I can't do that."

Jeff shook his head. "Then walk away. It's the kind thing to do."

Was it the kind thing to do? Was he being selfish in seeing what could come out of this intense chemistry he had with Chloe?

Yes.

Jeff Harper knew the truth—Nicolas sang about forever relationships but he had no idea how to make one last.

He didn't say another word. He stomped to his room and plopped down on the couch.

*Merda.* What was the right thing to do? He wanted Chloe Harper more than he'd wanted anyone in a long time. And a week would not be enough.

He thought back over all of the pretty faces in his past and realized that Jeff was right—Chloe was special. No one had come closer to being someone who could genuinely complete his life. She was the real deal, a woman who could be a forever girl, but could he be a forever man?

Chloe thought he had the right stuff for a long-lasting relationship, but he wasn't so sure he was capable of the kind of commitment she deserved.

He couldn't change who he was, even if part of him,

a big part, wanted to. He'd always be the poor, desperate boy struggling to support his family and make the world love him. He worked like the devil to keep the demons of poverty away but that meant making everyone else in his life a second or third priority. Finding space in his life to be fully present with Chloe in a real loving relationship, long-term? No, he couldn't see how to do it.

Jeff Harper was right. He should walk now.

So why wouldn't his legs move?

His cell rang. He looked around the room and re-membered he'd left it inside the drawer in the bedroom because Chloe had asked him to. It was just another sign that the woman was getting to him. When had he ever left his phone behind for anyone? And yet he hadn't thought about answering emails or taking calls all day.

"Yeah?" he answered.

"I've been texting all day. I thought you'd died for real this time," Tony, his former agent, complained. "Are you okay?"

"Never better. I disconnected for the day."

"Jeez, Nic. You've got to tell me when you are taking a break from reality. Just about gave me a coronary."

"You need to exercise more and eat less. So…what's up?"

"I was just checking in on you. Your office is driv-ing me nuts. You apparently disconnected from their calls, too."

"I did. Everyone deserves a vacation, Tony."

"Don't bite my head off—I'm just the messenger. So…how's the Harper property?"

Nicolas thought about all the beautiful spots Chloe

had shown him. His favorites were the ones where he got a taste of her lips to sweeten the view. *Deus*, she had been so beautiful standing on that ledge, looking out to sea. Like a goddess.

"Amazing. I'm going to sign the contract. The place is perfect for the show."

"You don't want to see the other two locations first?"

"No. I've seen everything I want and it's here." She was here. "And I may be staying a few more days to enjoy the area. It's a beautiful place for yoga."

There was a beat of silence. "Ah, no. Tell me this isn't about another woman. Is she the one teaching you yoga, making you sign the contract?"

Nicolas didn't say a word.

"Jeez, Nic. Lila is still out there smearing your name and you're getting it on with a stranger? What's the matter with you, man?"

She was no stranger. They'd only known each other for a few days, but he knew Chloe. It seemed like he'd known her forever.

"This lady is special, Tony. Nothing like Lila. She's genuine and sweet. Kind and thoughtful. She's one of a kind."

"Yeah, sure she is. They all are when they want something from you." Tony let out a sharp breath. "When are you going to grow up?"

That hurt. "I am trying to be a better man here."

"Really? 'Breathing in light and exhaling fears' and all that crap?"

Nicolas's heart skipped a beat. "What did you say?"

"Yoga brainwashing. Did you forget that I was taken

in by a yoga instructor once? A real babe. I thought I loved her." Tony snorted in disgust. "After I talked up her studio, sent some real big hitters her way, she dumped me like a sack of trash. She was a cold, callous man-eater."

Tony had complained about this yoga instructor before, but he'd been in love? It didn't seem possible. Tony dated; he didn't settle down. The women at Nicolas's music label complained that Tony hit on them all the time and were more than a little pleased when he'd been spurned by someone outside the music industry. They had, in fact, cheered about it.

Tony was still fuming about the yoga instructor. "The blue-eyed babe had my number. What a great actor she was."

A strange foreboding poked Nicolas in the solar plexus. "What was her name?"

"Chloe Harper."

His heart all but stopped. *No, no, no. Tony had loved Chloe?*

He heard Chloe's voice in his memory. *I moved here because I couldn't stand the fakeness. The superficiality. I'm striving for deeper relationships now.*

Was that true, or was she an actress after all? She'd supposedly used Tony to advance her yoga studio. Had she used Nicolas to get him to sign her father's contract? Had she taken him like she'd taken Tony?

If so, it was his own damn fault. He'd let his guard down and trusted her.

"Are you listening to me, Nicky? Don't sign your

life away. And stop sleeping with every woman who comes along."

The line went as dead as his pretty dreams.

Chloe woke with a start. Was that a slamming door?

She pulled her robe on and opened her own bedroom door. A package fell at her feet. She looked down the hall but was alone. Why hadn't Nicolas come to her room?

She turned the package over and saw a note.

Chloe,
Something came up. I had to go back to LA. I will call you.
NM
PS You did a great job making me fall in love with the place.

She opened the envelope and found her dad's contract. Signed. Nicolas agreed to having the show at Plunder Cove. She'd fulfilled her job. Dad was going to be proud of her for once.

She should be happy, but something told her that the "thing" that came up was all wrong.

# Nineteen

Nicolas had rented a car to drive back to LA. The long drive gave him time to think.

Tony had been in love with Chloe, which didn't surprise him in the least. Chloe was easy to love. But what had she felt for Tony?

Was Chloe a con artist? The conniving man-eater Tony said she was?

No, Nicolas couldn't believe it. Her lips, her sexy body, hadn't lied when Nicolas touched her. She'd let herself go with him, completely, wholly. He knew who Chloe Harper was at the core. She was a caring, real, wounded woman who was working on becoming her best self. She had risen above her lousy childhood and had helped others through her yoga and kindness.

She'd tried to help him rise above his lousy childhood, too. She hadn't failed. Her process was working. When he'd tried to live in the moment and to feel as intensely as she did, he learned to just…breathe.

While he was with her, he forgot about everything that had hurt him, everything that had led him to work way too hard and lose the music he'd once loved. It was an amazing thing to let some of the suffering go and to kick the heavy baggage he'd been carrying for twenty years to the side. In doing so, he'd connected with Chloe like he'd never connected with anyone. He was completely alive for the first time in his life. Sensations, colors, feelings, everything was beautiful when he was with her.

But it wasn't enough, was it?

He cared for her, was attracted to her, to everything about her. But love? He had no idea what true love was. How could he give something to her that was beyond his comprehension? It ripped him up when she'd cried after they'd made love the last time. Had she known the truth then—that he would never be the guy she hoped he'd become? Possibly.

It broke his heart that he wasn't a better guy. He wasn't good enough for Chloe Harper and never would be.

He knew who he was.

A man who'd done very little to help humanity. One who had performed no real acts of kindness. He'd dated lots of women but hadn't loved any of them. He wasn't a father. He had few real friends. If he'd learned anything the last few days, he finally understood that he needed to do better with his life. *Be* better.

Jeffrey Harper was right. Nicolas didn't deserve Chloe. Not now anyway. If he could work on himself, like she had worked on herself, maybe he could become the man he was supposed to be. A better man. In her search for deeper relationships, she had changed. He could, too.

Maybe.

Somehow.

He didn't expect her to wait for him. She should move on and find a man who was already worthy of her. She should grow the family she cared about so much. Chloe deserved that and more.

He drove on in the night, heading toward his dark, large home in Beverly Hills, feeling lonelier than he ever had in his life.

His cell phone buzzed with a text coming in. His heart sped up, hoping it was Chloe, but his mind wondered what he'd say if it was. He didn't have the courage to say goodbye to her yet, because a large part of him didn't want to let her go. As he came to a stoplight, the image that appeared on his screen was not the one he wanted to see.

*Lila.*

He didn't answer it. He didn't care why she was calling. He felt exactly nothing.

Driving through the night, he realized that he'd dodged a bullet as far as Lila was concerned.

His cell phone beeped again, and the screen lit up with Lila's text.

I made a huge mistake. I need you, Nicky. Call me. Please.

He shook his head and turned on the radio, catching the end of a song he loved. He'd produced it two years ago and it still made him smile. He hadn't been the singer or songwriter, but he knew in his heart that it wouldn't still be on the radio two years later if he hadn't been the producer. He let himself absorb the good feelings and enjoy them. Breathing it in. It had been a long time since he'd felt pride in his work. There was only one word to describe what had changed him.

*Chloe.*

"I'm living in the moment, sweetheart," he said softly. "Wish you were here."

When the song ended, the DJ's voice came on. "Our thoughts and prayers go out to Billy See. We all hope he gets better quickly."

Nicolas gripped the steering wheel. What happened to his drummer, his friend? Ex-friend.

He pulled off the freeway, picked up his cell phone and listened to Lila's voice mail.

"Hey, Nicky. I know you don't want to talk to me. I get it." She made a sound that reminded him of air squeaking out of a balloon. "I screwed up with you, with Billy. I'm so sorry." She was crying. "Billy and I had an argument and he got on his motorcycle… Oh, God. He hit a tree, Nicky. He's in the ICU, Cedars-Sinai. I can't… I don't have anyone… Please come."

He didn't hesitate. He texted back.

I'm about two hours out. Hang on. I'm coming.

When Nicolas didn't call the next day, Chloe got worried. She went to the hotel construction site to see

Jeff. He was behind the workmen's tape, talking to the foreman.

"Jeff, can I talk to you?" she called to her brother.

He lifted his finger and came out to see her. "What's up?"

"Have you heard from Nicolas?"

"Uh. Nope."

"He left in such a hurry. What did you tell him?"

"Me?" He had his guilty face on. "Great work, by the way. I'm glad he signed the contract. The show is really going to help us with publicity."

"I'm glad he chose our resort, too. But now he's gone and I have a feeling by the pinkness creeping up into your earlobes that you know why. Spill it, Jeffrey Davis."

"Ouch. My middle name, too? That sounds serious."

She crossed her arms.

"I know his type, Chloe. He's a player. You don't want a guy like him."

Oh, yes, she did. More than anything. "What did you say to him exactly?"

"That you are special and deserve a man who will love and cherish you for keeps. You are important to me, Chloe. To Matt and Dad, too."

She pressed her hand to her chest. "Wow, Jeff. That was really sweet." And it sounded suspicious. "Nicolas told you to say that, didn't he?"

"Doesn't mean it's not true. Seriously, Chloe, I love you. We all do. You are the glue in this family that makes it all stick together."

Tears filled her eyes. "Thank you. I think I knew

that, but I guess I needed to hear it out loud. You are a sweet brother." She hugged him.

He patted her back. "Yeah, really sweet. Keep that thought."

She looked up at him. "What else did you tell him?"

He rubbed the back of his neck, a typical nervous Jeff move. "After Nicolas and I had our little come-to-truth moment, I, uh, threatened to destroy him if he hurt you. You know, the usual brotherly love stuff."

"You wouldn't destroy him."

"Of course I would. If he hurt you, there would be nothing left of him. Matt feels the same way." Jeff paused. "Okay, fine. I might have told him he should leave, too."

A boulder dropped into her belly. "What? No, Jeff, you didn't!" She gave him a shove.

"Hey!"

"Why did you do that? I'm an adult. I can make my own choices with men. What is the matter with you?"

"Just listen to me for a second. What I said was just a shot across the bow, a warning. Guys get this stuff. Brothers have to say things like that to protect their little sisters. Everyone knows it."

She frowned. "Not me. No one has ever stood up for me like that before." Both Nicolas and Jeff had tried to protect her and yet here she was. Alone. "I don't understand. For the first time in my life, I *had* a boyfriend I really care about and now he is gone. Explain it to me."

"I'm sorry, sis. I really am, but he doesn't deserve you. That's why Medeiros left. You are far too good for him. He knows it. I know it. You should see it, too.

I suggested that if he couldn't do right by you, then he should leave immediately. It was the right thing to do. The kind thing."

She paced in front of him, her sandals kicking up dirt. "You had no right to do that, Jeff!"

"I was trying to protect you and look out for your feelings."

She threw her hands up. "I wish people would stop looking out for my feelings and just let me feel them! I'm getting him back."

"Don't call him, Chloe. Guys hate that."

"You are not the boss of me," she said, just as she used to do when she was a kid.

She stomped back to the house, determined to dial Nicolas's number as she went.

And she was ignoring how much she worried that Jeff was right.

But when she unlocked her phone, the morning news popped up and she saw an image of Nicolas with his arm wrapped tightly around Lila. The supermodel had her head nuzzled into his chest, like she belonged there. His other hand was lifted as if to shield her and block the photographer's shot.

*No, that...can't be!*

Chloe stared at her phone, not quite understanding what she was seeing, or not wanting to. The news media was wrong, that's all. They had to be using an old digital image from when Nicolas and Lila were a couple. She peered closely, studying Nicolas. He was still wearing the clothes he'd had on last night at their bonfire date. Chloe's heart beat so hard, she worried it would explode. She ripped her gaze from his gorgeous, sad eyes and read the first words of the article.

*Nicky M comforts Lila as Billy See remains in critical condition after his motorcycle slammed into a tree...*

Suddenly, she knew what "thing" kept Nicolas from her bed last night. Her chest shuddered on her inhale as she tried not to cry. She understood why Nicolas would be in the hospital, waiting to see if his friend—well, ex-friend—would pull through, but did he have to be holding Lila like that after what she did to him?

More importantly, would he let Lila go?

Chloe's heart thudded through a dread that felt as thick as quicksand.

Had she just lost her boyfriend to his ex-lover?

# Twenty

It was midmorning when RW got home. He didn't speak to anyone. He went straight into his den, opened his safe and pulled out a leather satchel.

"There you are," Claire said behind him. "We've all been looking for you, RW. Matthew was about to send out the Forestry's search-and-rescue team."

RW hid the satchel behind his back. "A man should be able to take a drive once in a while, Claire."

"Don't snap at me. I'm just saying I was worried. Are you okay?" She came closer.

He was shocked by the compassion on her face. When was the last time she'd looked at him with any feeling other than rage or disappointment? It set him back a step.

"Yeah. I'm fine. Just had business to take care of. No

one should've worried." Acting casual, he strode to the desk and put the satchel inside the drawer.

"That's what family does, RW."

*Family.* He would do anything for the people he loved. And everything. He'd lost sight of that when he was with Claire, or maybe he just hadn't gotten it then.

He got it now.

"Why are you still here, Claire?"

She crossed her arms, looking so much like Chloe that it was uncanny. "I told you. I'm not leaving."

"Really? Why not? You don't belong here." Another voice said behind them. RW's heart leaped at the sound.

"Angel." He pushed past Claire and had Angel in his arms before anyone said another word. He cupped her cheek and kissed her lips softly. "You came back."

"Let me see you." She ran her hands through his hair, as if drinking him in. A radiant smile lit up her face. Hell, he'd missed that smile, so much that he wanted her here no matter what kind of deals she'd made with Cuchillo.

"Who do you think you are?" Claire was suddenly standing behind them, poking Angel in the shoulder. "Aren't you the help?"

"Claire!" RW growled. "No, she's not the help."

For a moment he'd actually forgotten Claire was still in the room. He warned himself to tread lightly with Claire because she had the power to steal from RW the one thing he wanted most—Angel as his wife.

"Mom, what are you doing in here?" Chloe rushed in behind her mother. "Angel! You're back."

"Hi, sweet girl," Angel said to Chloe. "It's good to see you."

RW was surrounded by all of the women who had been important in his life. Right now, he just wanted one.

"Chloe, please take your mother outside. Or go to the restaurant. I will be meet you both later."

"Um, sure. Mom, let's go," Chloe gently took her mother's arm.

"I'm not a child that can be hushed and sent away. I asked you a question, Angel, or is it Juanita?" she asked, referencing the time Angel had spent running a café in Pueblicito under an assumed name when she was hiding from Cuchillo. "What are you doing in RW's room?" Claire demanded.

"Shouldn't I be asking you that question?" Angel faced Claire and trembled with rage. "I've spent years to repair the damage you've done, lady. Why don't you crawl back under the rock you came from and leave RW alone?"

Claire looked shocked. "How dare you speak to me that way. I belong here more than you do. Tell her, RW."

"Claire! That's enough," RW barked. Putting his hand on Angel's shoulder, he said softly, "Angel, darling, we need to talk."

"Talk about her? No, we do not." Angel lifted her chin and focused her rage on Claire. "You hurt him and left him when he needed you the most. You hurt your kids, too. Who does that? And now you're back to what? Take what you can from the family who is finally starting to live again? What sort of beast are you?"

"You don't know how it was," Claire yelled at her. "He wasn't like he is now. He was terrible."

"Mom! This is not a good idea. Please let it go," Chloe pleaded.

RW hated that his daughter had to see any of this. Hadn't he and Claire done enough damage to their kids?

"She's right." RW stepped between Angel and Claire. "I was terrible. No one should have had to put up with me back then. I didn't know how to stop the downward spiral. How to fix *me*. I'm sorry, Claire. I hope you will eventually forgive what I did to us. And Chloe, I swear I will spend the rest of my life making it up to you for ruining your childhood. I'm sorry, sweetheart."

Claire opened her mouth but no words came out. Chloe blinked as if she'd fallen through a hole like Alice in *Alice's Adventures in Wonderland*, which he used to read to her.

He faced Angel, cupping her cheek in his warm large hand. "I'm not that man anymore. I have changed because of you, Angel. You changed everything. Please don't leave again. I can't stand life without you."

"Oh, RW. I missed you so much." Angel turned her head and kissed his palm. "There's something I must tell you."

"I know. There's something I must tell you, too. Will you excuse us?" He then ushered his wife and daughter out the door.

"But—" Claire began.

"Later, Claire." He closed the door softly in his wife's face.

RW tugged Angel against his chest and wrapped his

arms around her. He kissed her deeply, treasuring her lips, her breath, the way she fit perfectly in his arms.

He'd missed her so much, it hurt. Kissing her now—knowing that she might not stay after he told her the truth—hurt, too. And yet he couldn't stop kissing her any more than he could stop his heart from beating. She was his drink, his drug, his life. After several long delicious minutes of reacquainting himself with her wonderful lips, he led her to the couch and sat next to her.

"Why is she here?" Angel asked.

He exhaled heavily. "She's my wife, Angel."

She blinked, cocked her head and studied his face. "You mean, she *was* your wife."

"Hell, in my mind everything about that woman is past tense, but legally..." He rubbed her soft skin. "She's still Mrs. Harper."

"You mean you're still married?" It physically hurt him when she scooted out of reach. Her posture was tense like she was about to bolt again.

"Not in my mind, no. I sent her the divorce papers long ago. I actually thought she'd signed them, but I didn't follow up. It seems stupid now, but that's the truth."

She chewed her lip. "You haven't been together for years. Why didn't she sign the papers?"

He closed the gap between them and pulled her legs into his lap. "She could have. It was obvious we were never going to be husband and wife again. Especially with how things ended between us. I'm not sure exactly why she hasn't signed. She continues to draw a healthy monthly income from our combined shares and never had to work a day in her life. That wouldn't change with a divorce."

Angel just shook her head. "And yet you and your children work very hard."

"I'll get her to sign the divorce papers. She must see that there is nothing more for her here. I'll explain it to her again. If I pay her enough money, she'll sign. I know she will." He pressed his forehead to hers. "Anyone with two eyes can see that I am in love with you."

"Oh, RW." Her eyes misted.

He got down on one knee. "Marry me, Angel. Please."

Her voice cracked as she insisted that he rise. "You're too good for me, RW. I'm not worthy of your love." She covered her mouth as if to keep the sadness inside. Softly she said, "You have no idea why I'm here."

He took her hand and held it to his chest. "You came back and that's all that matters."

She let out a deep breath. "I had to."

"Because Cuchillo sent you."

She went pale. "How? Why would you say that?"

"I know you went to see him. He could have killed you."

"I went to protect you, to protect Julia. And everyone here. I begged him to stop following me. I want to have a life, too, RW." She looked him in the eye. "A life with you."

He sucked in a breath. She was the only thing he wanted. "Marry me."

"I can't. Cuchillo will kill you if he knows how much I..." She bit her lip. "I just can't."

"How much you *what*?"

Her bottom lip trembled and it took all his strength not to kiss it still. "How much I love you, RW. With all my heart. You are the only man I have ever loved."

He pulled her into his lap and kissed her like he'd never kissed anyone. He poured his heartbreak, joy, fears, life and love into that kiss. He never wanted to stop.

She was the one who pulled away.

"Don't you see? Cuchillo won't let us be happy together. He will kill you just to spite me. I can't lose you, RW. That's why I've stayed away for so long. I'm afraid of what he will do to the people I love."

"First off, you can't lose me. You are a part of my heart, the oxygen in my blood, my every thought and everything I do. I'm not really me without you." He kissed her temple. "Second off, Cuchillo will leave you alone once you give him what he asked for."

She frowned. "How do you know about that?"

"I was there. I heard his demands."

"RW! You went to see Cuchillo? How could you put yourself at risk like that? He could have killed you."

"For the same reason you went. To make it safe for you to live without fear. And I know why you came back—to rob me."

She stood up. "No. I told him that, but I won't take anything from you, RW. I can't."

"You are partially right. The only thing you can take from me is my undying love and devotion. I expect you to take as much of that as you can handle. In regards to what Cuchillo wants…" He rose and went to the desk drawer and pulled out the satchel. "I'm fully prepared to *give* you what you need. Here. These are stock options that should be more than enough to take to the bastard and call it square."

"No." She pushed the satchel toward him. "I need only you, RW. I don't need your money. I'm nothing like Claire."

"I know that, sweetheart. But you have to pay that bastard, or we'll never be free of him."

"I may have another way. Please sit by me. I have a story to tell."

He sat but his heart was pounding. If she didn't take his money, Cuchillo would always be lurking in the shadows, keeping them apart.

"I told you a little bit about my past, but I want you to hear everything. You need to know who you want to marry and what I did."

Her face was stricken with worry. Did she think he'd change his mind? He knew who Angel was. The past didn't matter to him. He linked his fingers with hers and held on.

"I ran away from home when I was thirteen. My parents had passed and I didn't like my sisters bossing me around. I thought I was tough enough to live on the streets without any family." She shook her head. "I didn't have a clue. My nickname was *Ladronita*, Little Thief. I took food and clothing only, to feed myself and other runaway kids. It was all about survival. Then Cuchillo saw me and invited me into his gang. He taught me how to become a better thief. I was a member of his family then, his girl."

She looked into RW's eyes as if expecting condemnation. She'd find none there. "You have nothing to be ashamed of. You were a child who was used and mistreated by adults."

She nodded. "Still, I knew better. I thought I had it all under control, until I saw with my own eyes what Cuchillo was capable of. He was no hero, no father figure. He was an evil man." She shuddered. "I didn't want to raise my baby in that world. I ran away when I was several months pregnant."

Her hands trembled in his. "I took Cuchillo's baby from him, to protect her and myself. But that was not all I took." She dug around in her purse and pulled out a long jewel-encrusted knife.

"Whoa. What is that?" RW asked.

"Cuchillo's treasured legacy." She turned it around so he could get a good look. "His grandfather gave it to him in Colombia. It was symbolically important because the man who wielded the ancient blade was supposed to hold the family's power in his hand. The legend told through the generations is that the blade was taken from a pirate who dared to attack the family's ship."

He took the knife from her and studied it in the light. "It looks like it might have come from Spain. I have gold coins, doubloons, from the 1500s that resemble the gold used in this knife. The jewels embedded in the hilt are worth a fortune, too, each one. But—" he looked at Angel "—some of the jewels are missing."

"I know." She was pale again. Her voice was soft, her eyes full of fear. "I took a ruby and an emerald out years ago and hocked them to buy the café in Pueblicito. And then to pay for Julia's college education, even though she didn't know the money came from me. It was the only way I knew how to pay for everything."

His heart went as cold as ice. "If Cuchillo finds out you did this to his family's heirloom—"

"He'll kill me, RW. For that alone. But also for stealing his daughter. And once the news spreads, his grandfather will send someone to kill him. That's why Cuchillo is so desperate to get the jeweled knife back."

Silence filled the room.

RW's mind started spinning with ways to fix this mess.

She put her hand on his arm. "That's why I had to come here. Not to rob you, but to ask for a loan to buy the jewels back. The new owners will sell once I tell them the history. No one in their right mind would steal from Cuchillo's grandfather. Except me, of course." Her lips actually quirked with self-deprecating humor. At a time like this? God, she was amazing. "Once I return the knife to Cuchillo—and allow him to meet Julia—then maybe, hopefully, he'll leave us all alone."

RW hated the idea of her dealing with that killer again. "That's a big gamble, Angel."

She sighed. "What choice do I have?"

"Let me think on it. For now, you're staying with me," he growled.

"That's not necessary."

"Oh, babe, it's necessary. I have big plans for you tonight." He hadn't forgotten that she'd said she loved him. He'd been waiting years to hear those words from someone who meant them.

Tipping her chin up, he gazed into her beautiful, expressive face and swore to himself that he'd make her smile again. "Plus, I haven't heard an answer to my proposal."

"I'm not giving you a yes until I know for sure that Cuchillo is not going to come after us."

"I'll figure that out. For now, let me make you happy."

"You do, RW. You always do." She wrapped her hand around his neck and pulled his lips to hers.

# Twenty-One

Nicolas and Lila were in the waiting room, desperate for a doctor, nurse or anyone to come out and give them Billy's status after his operation. Nicolas got up and bought two cups of coffee.

"Here. Drink."

Lila took one from him with a shaky hand. "It feels like forever."

"Yeah. If someone doesn't come out soon, I'll go see what's going on."

He sat across from her. "How are you holding up?"

She threw her hands in the air. "I'm dying here. Oh, Nicky, the last thing I said to him was...terrible."

He didn't ask, didn't want to know. She'd said terrible things about him, too. Lila was volatile and her mouth could get the best of her. "Billy knows you care about him. Just let it go."

She sipped her coffee, thinking. After a long moment, Lila pushed her hair out of her eyes. "I must look a fright."

Even with little sleep and maximum stress, she was supermodel beautiful. But he'd learned that he preferred a genuine beauty. One that got more and more appealing every second he was with her. He'd seen a true beauty and held her in his arms.

*My Chloe.*

"You look fine, Lila. Besides, who cares? You're in the ICU waiting room, not on a catwalk. Give yourself a break."

"Wow. You've never said anything like that to me before. You're...different," she said. "Calmer. More— I don't know—centered."

He grinned. "Yes. I am."

She tipped her head and waited for him to say more. He didn't. It felt wrong to talk about Chloe with his ex. Besides, he wasn't sure how to explain all the ways that she'd changed him.

"Well, whatever you are taking or doing, keep it up. Calmer looks good on you." She leaned forward. "I'm glad you're here, Nicky. I wouldn't have blamed you if you had told me to take a hike. What I said about you during that television interview... I didn't mean it."

"Words are powerful. Important. They mean things, Lila."

*And so do lyrics.*

Suddenly he understood why writing music was so

important to him. Why he'd pushed it aside for so long. Words touched people, connected them, made the listener feel emotions, life. He'd been trying to hide from all of that, from all of the pain he'd felt as a child.

Chloe *had* changed him.

Now he wanted to feel everything. With her.

"I know. I'm going to try to be better. I promise," Lila said.

*Better.*

The word clicked in his brain and linked up with the familiar tune that played frequently in his head. It was the melody that had come to him in a nightmare in which Chloe had stood shoulder to shoulder with him as he faced his fears. It was the first nightmare in which he wasn't alone. The melody was intriguing, pulsing, vibrant—just like Chloe.

*My Pirate Girl.*

The title came to him like a flash of light, sending a tingle of hope up his spinal cord.

*"Merda!"* he said. It was perfect.

"What is it?" Lila asked.

"Nothing," he said. He wasn't ready to share the only song he'd titled in years. And he didn't want to push too hard to find the lyrics. He was afraid they might not come, so instead he said, "I've got some work to do. Mind if I do it while we wait?" he pointed toward his laptop.

She lifted her palms up. "No, of course not. I know you must have tons of work. Go for it."

He grabbed his computer and checked his email.

He had one from RW Harper. His heart pounded as he opened it. Was Chloe all right?

"Nicolas, I am excited about the prospect of producing your show on my property. I have one more caveat that I believe will benefit us both. Please return to Plunder Cove so that I can show you a gem that will make you a very wealthy man."

Nicolas stared at the screen. Leave it to RW Harper to try to negotiate another deal after the first one was done. *Sorry, Harper, but that's a big no.* If he returned to Plunder Cove, he wouldn't be able to keep his hands off Chloe. And he'd hurt her. Again. He couldn't do it. It was better for her that she believed he didn't miss her "kiss me" lips, better if she went on with her life.

As he needed to do. Someday.

He still had several contestants to listen to for the show, so he put his earphones on, but what he played was Chloe's last voice mail. She'd left several and had hung up without a message a few times, too. He hadn't returned any of her calls. He couldn't because he was too weak. If he spoke to her, he'd hop in his car and drive up the coast to Plunder Cove. He would ruin her grand plan for a good life. It was better to not call and let her get over him.

"Hey. It's me." She sounded tired. "I won't call again because I know you won't return it. I get it. You've moved on. If Lila makes you happy, then… I'm happy. I only want the best for you." She paused. "I'm going to miss you." She made a sound that resembled a forced laugh that got clogged in her throat. "We were good for each other. I truly believe that. Because of you, I know what I am capable of feeling. But, uh, I'm not going to talk about that, because this call is awkward enough. Just…find love, okay? You deserve it. Goodbye, Nicolas."

His chest felt tight. His mind rolled with sadness because he knew he'd hurt her, even though he'd tried not to.

He'd left the only chance he had at finding love, because he was scared he'd ruin it. He hadn't called Chloe back, because he was a *burro*. He wanted the best for her, too, and Nicolas Medeiros obviously wasn't it. Not even close.

*Adeus,* Chloe.

He closed his eyes and envisioned Chloe Harper one last time. It was sweet torture. He could smell her fragrance, taste her honey, her lips, her sweet skin. Her voice was the music in his head. Her words, the lyrics. Her intensity, sincerity, depth, realness, kindness and goodness all poured over him. He imagined her swimming naked in the moonlight, the phosphorescence glowing around her slender figure, and wished that just once he could have bodysurfed the Pacific with her. He pictured her dancing in his arms and let her music play in his head. He was overwhelmed with feelings. He opened his eyes.

He opened his notes file, but instead of typing lyrics on a page, he let his fingers pour out all the emotions he felt about Chloe. He could barely type fast enough to keep up with the upbeat melody dancing in his brain. When he was done, he stared at the screen in utter surprise. On his computer monitor was the first song he'd written in more than a decade.

And it was good! No, not good. The song was great because it sounded like Chloe.

His heart pounded hard, for he knew, really knew, that this was a hit. This was the one he couldn't find in all the years that had come before Chloe. But more than that, he had laid out the truth in black-and-white, for even a *burro* to see.

"What just happened?" Lila asked him.

He took his headphones off. "What?"

"I was watching you work and the look on your face! I've never seen that expression on anyone. What are you watching on your computer?"

He swallowed. "A guy in love."

Before he had to say anything more, a doctor walked up to Lila. "Mr. See is out of surgery and asking for you."

Lila rose to her feet. "Billy is okay?"

"Yes. He's going to need time to recover and some rehab, but he is out of danger," the doctor said.

"Oh, my God. Thank you!" She kissed the doctor on the cheek and blew an air kiss toward Nicolas. "My man is going to be okay."

"Go to him. Tell him I hope he feels better fast," Nicolas said. "And to take care of you."

"Thank you." Lila almost ran down the hall.

Nicolas smiled. "Goodbye, Lila." He didn't think he'd ever see her or Billy again. He was at peace with that. He hadn't loved Lila. Or anyone before his short but sweet visit to Plunder Cove. He could appreciate the difference between lust and love now.

He grabbed his stuff, jumped to his feet and rushed out of the hospital. He had a long drive ahead of him. He hoped he wasn't too late to prove that he was, in fact, long-lasting material.

# Twenty-Two

RW invited Claire to meet him at the gazebo. It was a spot they used to share for quiet moments away from the kids and staff. RW recalled the times they would meet here at sunset to talk, drink cocktails and—when they'd been on happier terms—have a romantic moment.

It was a lifetime ago. And he was a different man.

"Our old place," Claire said as she climbed the steps.

"Come. Join me." He made room for her on the bench. "There is something serious I need to discuss with you."

"Let me guess. Angel, right? Is this—" she waved her hand "—*thing* with her really all that serious?"

"You have no idea." He watched her take a seat next to him—two married strangers. "I've been trying to figure out why you didn't sign the divorce papers. We haven't been any sort of married couple for years. Why do you still want to be tied to me? Is it all about the money?"

She blinked fast like she might cry. This was new. He'd seen Claire rage, scream, throw things at his head, but he couldn't remember ever seeing Claire shed a tear.

"I know you don't want me. Except for our early years, when the kids were babies, no one has ever wanted or needed me."

He reached for her hand and took it. "That's not true."

She lifted her chin but did not pull her hand away. "It is. I admit I'm not the easiest person to be with. But you and the kids—you're my family. The only one I have. Without you, I'm simply—" she lifted her shoulders and dropped them heavily "—me."

He chuckled softly. "There has never been anything simple about you, Claire. And for the record, I am not the easiest to be with either. I know, huge news flash."

She tried not to smile but didn't succeed. "You are funnier now, too. Why did I miss out on all the good stuff?"

"Because we were wrong for each other. It took Angel coming into my life for me to see that. For me to want to seek redemption and happiness. I want all of that for you, too."

She wagged her finger at him. "You just want me to sign the divorce papers. Nice try but I will not sign over my family to that...that...woman."

He sat back, finally getting it. Claire needed the same

thing he did—loved ones, people who understood and took care of one another. Family. It all made sense now.

"No matter what happens, you are still the mother of my children. No one can take that away from you. You'll still be a part of this family. I swear that to you, Claire. You are part of me, part of them. You don't need to be Mrs. Harper to be one of us."

She blinked and the tears fell. "Really?"

"Yes, really."

She dabbed at her eyes. "You'll invite me to the weddings? Baby showers? Birthdays?"

His kids were going to kill him. "Sure."

She nodded slowly, letting his words sink in.

He glanced around, making sure they were really alone, and then he told her about Cuchillo and about how he planned to take the man down. She sat quietly but her eyes were wide and her body rigid. He couldn't read her expression.

"So, this is where you step up and prove you care more about our children than you do money, Claire."

"Our children have always come first!"

"No, not always."

She wiped her cheek. "I've been a lousy mom, but I swear I want the chance to change. I love them."

"Good. Because my plan means giving up a lot of money to protect our family—stock options that are worth quite a lot now."

He'd bought the stock as the precursor to a hostile takeover. But the takeover hadn't happened, because Angel had mellowed him. How would the shareholders respond when they found out a Colombian gang owned 15 percent of the company?

"You're just going to give him the shares?" Claire asked.

"As payment. He must sign a restraining order to not come within a hundred miles of any of us again."

She glanced over his shoulder. "Including Angel?"

"Especially Angel. I want her to live without fear." RW would give Cuchillo more money than the man had ever dreamed of, but only with a signed contract and no more threats. If he saw even a shadow that reminded him of Cuchillo, he'd make sure Cuchillo's grandfather received a very broken knife.

RW let out a deep breath. "But you are still my wife. And half owner of all of my assets. You have a say here. Do I have your consent to protect our children and grandson?"

She was silent for only a beat. "Of course, you do. I'm still their mother."

RW started to step away.

"Wait!" She wrestled her wedding ring off her finger. "Here." She put it in his palm. "I'll sign your papers. And you can sweeten the pot with this. It's worth—"

"I know how much it's worth, Claire." He took the ring, remembering the night he'd slipped it on her finger. "Thank you."

He had a family to protect.

# Twenty-Three

Chloe stripped down to her swimsuit and went for a swim in the ocean. She hoped the salt water would wash away her tears.

God, she missed Nicolas. He and his not-so-ex-girlfriend had popped up all over the internet. Some in the media said they had married in the hospital while Billy was in a coma. Others were reporting that Lila was carrying Nicky's baby already. Chloe didn't believe the reports—not really—but something was going on with Lila, because he hadn't called. The speculation, combined with the silence, was brutal.

She swam hard, her arms and legs driving her further out to sea until a sound made her lift her head from the water. She flipped over on her back and listened. Someone was calling her name. On the shore a figure waved at her. Her heartbeat sped up. Wiping the salt water out of her eyes, she squinted and realized it wasn't the man she wanted so desperately to see. It was a woman. Chloe reversed her direction and headed for the shore.

As she got closer, she realized the woman was her mother. *What now?* She kept swimming, focusing on keeping her strokes long, equal, breathing on both sides. She lifted her head again and saw that her mother wasn't alone on the beach.

*Uh-oh.* Angel stood beside her mom, close, nearly shoulder to shoulder.

Chloe kicked harder to head off the explosion that was about to happen on the sand. She lifted her head again and saw Julia and Michele walking toward the other two women. There was some sort of party going on and they all seemed to be waiting for her to get out of the water. Her mother lifted a towel for Chloe.

"Uh, what's going on?" Chloe said as she quickly wrapped up.

"It's your dad—" Angel began.

"And Matt and Jeff," Julia added.

Chloe's gaze swung from face to face. All the women were worried. "You guys are freaking me out. What happened?"

Her mother was the one who answered. "RW went to make a deal with Cuchillo, and the boys insisted on going with him."

"Oh, no. Didn't anyone stop them?" Chloe asked.

"They have to do this or the danger will never end." Claire's gaze was on Angel. "We're Harpers. And we take care of our own. We won't stand for a threat to any of us. Angel, you are one of us."

"*Dios mio.* Thank you." Angel reached out and pulled Claire into her arms. The two women hugged.

Chloe's jaw dropped. She looked at Julia and Michele, and they were just as flabbergasted as she was. How did this happen?

"My heart is not going to beat properly until they return. Let's go to the bar," Michele said.

"Cuchillo!" RW called out.

He was back at the compound, not hiding in the bushes. He saw men on the roof and suspected they were armed. He knew he was a sitting duck and hoped that Cuchillo would prove good to his word about meeting him to negotiate. "Have your men stand down."

"*Baja tus armas,*" a deep voice commanded from inside. "How do I know you have my family's legacy?"

"You'll have to trust me, just as I will trust you," RW said. He kept coming but motioned for his sons to stay behind him. "I will keep it safe unless you cross me."

"You have the payment with you?" Cuchillo asked.

RW lifted a satchel for all to see. "It's all here."

"Open the door," Cuchillo commanded.

A floodlight momentarily blinded RW while he was frisked. He knew he was clean. Matt and Jeff followed behind him.

"All right, Harper. Come on in. Welcome to my home. I'm sure it is nothing like your mansion."

RW didn't spend much time checking out the scenery. His eyes were pinned to the muscular middle-aged man puffed up before him and staring him down with dark, menacing eyes. "Cuchillo."

"I've got to hand it to you, Harper. Not many men would have the *cajones* to come here. Not sure if you are brave or stupid."

RW stared right back, unflinching. "Call me determined. Now, sign the restraining order and you can take the money, and Angel's debts will be paid in full. But I'll be watching. If I see even a hint that you or your gang is within a hundred miles of my family, you will pay. I've wiped out competitors far greater than you."

Cuchillo grinned. "I can see why she likes you, Harper. I will agree to your deal but I want one more thing. I want my daughter."

RW mentally begged Matt to stand down. He knew Matt would never put Julia in danger, not even to meet the father she'd never known. "Your daughter is not part of this bargain. She is safe and happy where she is. You need to let her be. Trust me. I know a thing or two about screwing up a person's life. I'm a father who has made mistakes, too. And I am working night and day to fix them. Redemption. Forgiveness. Striving to make things better for my family. That's what makes a man worthy to be called a father. You wouldn't understand."

"I understand family," Cuchillo snarled. "I want to know my daughter. Is that so wrong?"

"Is this the sort of life you want for her?" RW waved his hand around. "You're selfish."

Cuchillo didn't respond with words, but his dark eyes flashed with anger. RW had touched a nerve with the insult. Good, he was going to grind that nerve under his heel and make the man feel the truth. "A father takes care of his daughter and works to give her more than what he has. It should always be about her. A better life, a better world, far more love and kindness, for her. Not you. Her. Don't you want to be a good dad?"

RW had hurt his children in so many ways. He'd nearly broken them, but thank God his sons and daughter were Harpers. They were stronger than he was. They were survivors, fighters, lovers.

"How would I know how to be a good dad?" Cuchillo huffed, rising to his feet. "Angel took that chance away from me."

"She did what was best for your child. Saving her from a life of crime and fear. Angel raised your daughter in a place filled with love and friends. She grew up strong but not fearful. Cherished. Wouldn't you have wanted that for her?"

Cuchillo's eyes narrowed. "You know my daughter."

RW wouldn't lie. "I love her like a daughter. She is a part of my family now. Protected. So, do we have a deal, or will it be a war?"

RW saw what he hoped he'd see—Cuchillo blinked. He seemed to be thinking of his daughter instead of himself for once. "*Sí*. We have a deal."

As RW handed his enemy the satchel, he noticed Cuchillo's body language. Despair. RW knew how that felt.

"Let's rock and roll, Dad," Matt said.

"In a minute," RW said. "I have something else for Cuchillo."

RW raised his arm and chucked a silver object. Cuchillo caught it just as his men picked up their guns.

Cuchillo studied the object. "A phone?"

"It's a burn phone. If your daughter wants to talk to you, she can. You won't be able to trace its location."

Surprise lit up Cuchillo's features. "Why did you do this?"

"Because I know how it feels. Sometimes you want to hear your kid's voice to make sure she's safe. Happy."

Cuchillo nodded, his eyes watery. "You take care of my girl."

He nodded. "Remember our deal. Don't cross me."

He turned his back on the guns and forced his legs to walk steadily to the car. Once they got inside, Matt floored it. No one said a word or even inhaled for a few seconds.

"Hey, Dad?" Matt said, his voice soft.

"Yeah?" RW stared at the road ahead of them.

"That was seriously badass."

"Dad, you were amazing back there," Jeff agreed.

RW looked at both of his boys and grinned. "Your old man still has it in him, huh?" Then he touched both of their shoulders. "Thanks for the backup, boys. Let's go home. Our ladies are waiting for us."

# Twenty-Four

It was the night of the grand opening of the restaurant. Chloe was excited for Jeff and Michele, and thrilled that Angel and Dad were attending together. Chloe's mother was there, too. Things were as they should be.

Almost.

Nicolas was supposed to be here with her—dancing, eating and loving the night away. He hadn't returned her calls or texts. She'd resigned herself to the belief that she'd never hear from him again. It broke her heart. Just when she decided to put herself out there again, the man of her dreams decided she wasn't worth the effort. It hurt.

But she had discovered what she needed to know about herself. She'd learned that she could fall in love, quickly, deeply if she let herself feel. If she appreciated every moment as it came and didn't worry too much about the future she could love herself, and build a good life with a man.

Nicolas had shown her she was worthy of love, even if he couldn't be the man to provide it. For that realization, she was grateful. It was time to retire her promise to stay away from men and start dating again. Maybe, eventually, she'd even fall in love.

She put on her favorite cinnamon-red gown and her velvet-and-crystal stilettos. Generally, she was more comfortable in yoga pants and a T-shirt, but every now and then she really enjoyed wearing a ball gown and four-inch heels. Instead of pulling her hair up into a twist or into braids, she left her hair down. The curls that usually annoyed her, or got in the way while she was working, were loose about her face.

The restaurant looked fantastic. Torches lit up every pathway. A line of cars was coming up the drive and a band was already playing in the great hall. Jeff's camera crew from his old show were filming for commercials. Chloe smiled. They were doing this. Patrons were going to see how wonderful Michele's food was, enjoy Jeff's brilliant architectural designs and get a sneak peek of the new resort they all were creating. Finally.

"Wow, you look beautiful." Jeff kissed her cheek at the entrance.

"Don't sound so surprised. I can wear something other than yoga pants sometimes." She nudged him in the ribs. "You look handsome yourself. Tuxedos always look fabulous on Harper men."

Matt joined them and snagged a basket of steaming

bread and a dipping sauce as a server passed by. "Huge crowd. You ready to do our thing?"

"No. Not ever. I can't believe my dumb brothers roped me into this!"

"Us? It was Dad. He was the one who thought the singing Harper trio would add to the 'family image' of the place," Jeff said.

She held out her trembling hand. "I'm shaking already."

"Maybe you're hungry. Want a roll before we go on?" Matt offered her the bread basket.

"No, thanks. I'm too nervous to eat." She pressed her belly. "Hope I don't get sick up there."

"You won't. Breathe in light, exhale your fears," Jeff joked.

She slugged him.

Matt shook her shoulder. "Come on, it'll be fun. You only have to play your guitar in the first one."

"First?" Her eyes went wide. "There's more than one?"

"Maybe."

Jeff and Matt both laughed and dragged her up onstage, in front of the crowd. She was shaking all over. How had Nicolas ever done this?

RW picked up the mic. "Welcome, everyone. We are honored that so many of you came out to celebrate the grand opening of Plunder Cove with us. You are all in for a treat. Our chef, Michele Harper, is world-renowned and my personal favorite. She is busy right now, but later I will bring her out for a round of well-deserved applause." People applauded anyway. "Jeff here has done an amazing job getting the restaurant up and running in such a short time. The hotel is coming along well, too. Please check out the plans before you leave. This place is my home. It has been in the family for centuries, and now I want to share it with you all. My kids—Matt, Jeff and Chloe—have prepared a little something for you. Relax, eat and enjoy."

Nicolas walked into the restaurant as RW introduced Chloe and her brothers.

Nicolas stood off to the side of the crowd behind the Harper's table. Angel, Julia and little Henry were seated and preparing for the show. He looked at the small stage and his heart did a weird stumbling race in his chest when he saw her. She looked amazing in that red dress.

But something was wrong. She seemed pale and she struggled a bit to take the guitar out of the case.

"Come on, *amor*. You've got this," he said softly.

Angel turned her head. She'd heard him.

Up onstage, Matt took the mic. "In case you were wondering where all the pirates went, this is a little ditty about a pirate who turns forty far too late to enjoy the bounty. It's Dad's favorite song."

RW gave them a thumbs-up and went back to the family table. On the way, his eyes locked with Nicolas's. The man's smile was wise, as if he knew something Nicolas couldn't fathom. Nicolas dipped his head in acknowledgment and turned his focus back to the stage.

Matt sang the first part of the ballad. His voice wasn't bad. Jeff sang the next section. He too had a nice singing voice. When the two sang together, the song was actually good. Chloe played the guitar like a champ and sang the backup softly. She didn't have a mic, so no one could hear her. Nicolas smiled. She didn't have a thing to worry about.

When the song ended, the crowd roared with applause. Chloe blinked and a crooked grin covered her face. She seemed relieved to have the job done. Nicolas whistled.

"Encore! Encore!" The crowd chanted.

Jeff took the mic. "We do have one more, if we can convince my sister to sing the song she wrote for me when we were kids. How about it, Chloe?"

The crowd chanted her name. All the color drained from Chloe's face. She stared into the audience like an animal caught in the fast lane on the freeway.

"Look at me," Nicolas said.

Even though she couldn't hear him, her gaze swung over the crowd. She swallowed hard and picked up the guitar again.

Jeff situated the mic in front of her and motioned to the crowd to quiet down.

There was a painfully long moment when Chloe didn't move, didn't make a sound. Nicolas knew all about public humiliation and didn't want her to suffer through it. He could rescue her by offering to sing the new song he wrote. He'd wanted to give it to Chloe in private, but this would work, too. He started to go, but RW put a hand on his shoulder, stilling him.

And Chloe started to play.

The first chords on her guitar were simple, childlike, but when she opened her mouth and sang, it was as if

Nicolas heard light and sunshine. Hope. Her voice was sweet with a crackle of rasp. He'd never heard anything quite so pure. So unique. His mouth was open when he turned to look at RW.

"Her voice is amazing, isn't it?" RW said.

*Amazing* wasn't the word. He'd never heard anything like it. He listened with awe as Chloe sang to him, through him. She touched him, lifted him to heights he'd never experienced. He'd never been transported like this with his clothes on. The lyrics weren't bad either. Holy hell, she'd written them as a child?

When the song ended, the crowd roared. Nicolas was almost too stunned to move. RW rose to his feet and Nicolas snapped out of his trance, or whatever the hell she'd put him in, and applauded, too.

RW pulled him away from the table and into a quieter alcove. "What do you think? Can you get your label to sign her?"

Nicolas blinked. He still felt off balance, stunned by Chloe's singing voice. "What?"

"Sign her. Give her a music contract. Whatever you call it. Just give her the break that she needs."

Realization dawned. "*Chloe* is the gem you wanted me to see?"

"Of course. Why else would I have requested you come to stay for a week? I wanted you to see how great she is."

Nicolas should have felt used and betrayed; instead he felt...thankful. "You arranged this whole thing...for me to produce your daughter's music?"

"Hell, yeah, son. I owe my little girl. It's my fault

she isn't out on tour and at the top of the music charts right now. She used to sing all the time, nonstop. It was her greatest joy. But I got tired of the noise—can you believe that? My beautiful little girl with her heavenly voice. It's my fault. My sins knew no bounds. I'm trying to fix it. All of it. Please help me make amends to my little girl."

Nicolas couldn't stop his lips from rising. Harper was a sneaky bastard, but he also loved his daughter. Chloe was going to be so happy when she knew the truth. "Have you told her any of this?"

"Not yet. I'm steeling myself for how she's going to take it." RW ran his hand through his hair, nervously. "But it doesn't matter if she hates me for this setup I arranged with you because a father gives his children what they need."

"What they need," Nicolas said. Was he what Chloe needed? *Deus*, he hoped she thought so after he had been avoiding her for days.

RW went on, "For Matt, it was the family I took away and all the planes he can fly, for Jeff it was a chance to build the best resort ever and the chef of his dreams, and now it is Chloe's turn. I want to give her what she needs and that is you, Nicolas."

Nicolas was stunned. It sounded like RW meant she needed Nicolas as a man and a music producer. "Just to be clear, Chloe didn't know you had her work with me so that I could make her a famous singer?"

RW snorted. "Son, do you know anything about women? Of course not. But I have to tell you that I didn't expect you to fall in love with her."

Nicolas shook his head. "Why the hell not? Are you insane? She's perfect, amazing and gorgeous. She's..." He couldn't think of enough words to truly describe her. "She's Chloe. And let me tell you something, Mr. Harper. You hurt her again, with even one hint that she is less than absolutely perfect in any way, and you will have me to deal with. Got it?"

The man actually smiled. "Go tell her that, son."

His heart hit the tiles. "I don't deserve her. I hurt her. She can do so much better."

RW chuckled. "As my grandson, Henry, says, 'no doy.' But if you don't try to make it up to her, you'll never know, will you?"

"Know what?"

"What it feels like to be alive." He turned to Angel. "Dance with me, my love."

"Dad looks like he's having fun dancing with Angel. Hell must be loaded with ice cubes," Matt said.

Chloe snorted. "I've got to see that."

She rose up on her tiptoes to see over the crowd but it was no good. The place was packed. She went around the edge of the great hall and sure enough, RW Harper was slow dancing with Angel. The two of them looked like they were the only people on the planet.

"Way to go, Dad," she said to herself.

"Can I have this dance," a voice said behind her, sending delicious shivers up her back.

Chloe was too afraid to turn around and yet she was incapable of stopping herself.

"Nicolas!"

"*Droga*, you look so good, *gata*."

He did, too. Harper men weren't the only ones who looked great in a tuxedo.

His gaze warmed her down to her toes. "Wow. Your hair is down." He lifted a stray curl off her cheek. "So beautiful."

She sucked in a breath and found her words. "You're here."

"Yes, *gata*."

"I didn't think I'd ever see you again. You didn't return my calls."

His gaze temporarily dropped to his feet. Embarrassed? And then his dreamy eyes met hers. "I was involved with a situation…"

"A situation." She swallowed hard. "I know. I read about Billy See. Is he okay?"

"He's going to be. He's got a lot of physical therapy in his future but he got lucky. Not many people hit a tree on their motorcycles and survive."

"That's good." She wanted to ask about Lila, but didn't want to hear about her.

"There's another reason I didn't call."

"Oh?" Her heart was pounding. *Don't say Lila.*

"I had something to tell you and thought I should do it in person." The fact that he seemed nervous scared her more than anything else. She braced herself for bad news.

"You are a special lady, Chloe. In such a short period of time, you changed me. I would never have believed it could be done." He caressed her cheek slowly. "I am so grateful."

She could hear the *but* coming. She sucked in a breath. "It's okay, Nicolas. You don't have to do this. I get it. You didn't have to drive all the way back here to say goodbye. I've done the 'it's not you, it's me' speech enough times to know what comes next."

"Like with Tony?"

She frowned. "Tony?"

"Tony Ricci. My friend who used to be my agent. Did you love him?"

"No, I didn't. I tried, but…he was someone who made me feel okay for a while, until I realized I was lonelier with him than when I was alone. Does that make sense?"

"Yes. It does. More than I'd like to admit."

"So, that's why you came back. To ask me about Tony? Sorry I hurt him. I just didn't know how to love anyone…then."

"Then?"

Her mind was spinning. "Nicolas, why are you here?"

"I don't care that Tony loved you. I'm just glad you don't love him." He wrapped one of her loose hairs around his finger and leaned in. "There's so much I want to tell you, but I can't think straight with you so close. Please, *gata*, dance with me. I have been dying to touch you. Let's dance first, talk later."

She offered her hand and when his fingers sealed around hers, her whole body sighed. It felt good to touch him. Like home.

She led him to the center of the dance floor, next to her dad, and next to Matt and Julia.

"Hey, look. It's Mr. Fast Hips. Can't wait to see what

you've got, bro," Matt said just as he spun Julia under his arm.

"I showed him the music video and now he's trying to out-dance a seventeen-year-old boy," Julia explained. "Don't challenge him to a salsa dance-off, or this pregnant lady will have to sit down."

Chloe laughed. "My brother and Julia are the resident king and queen of the dance floor."

Nicolas nodded to both of them but put his hands on her. "The only queen I see is you. *Deus*, I missed you."

He held her close, his cheek to hers. They swayed softly to the beat. Everyone else in the room disappeared. His breathing in her ear both set her aflame and calmed her nerves. She was fully aware of every place his body touched hers.

There was that feeling again. *Home.*

"I heard you sing," he said.

Her cheeks heated. "Oh, God. Really? I'm so embarrassed. Sorry you had to hear that."

He tipped her chin up and looked her in the eye. "You have no idea how good you are, do you?"

She snorted. "Right."

"Chloe, this is no joke. I could make you a star."

She pressed her head to his chest. "I don't need to be a star, Nicolas." *I just need you.*

She had no idea why Nicolas was here or if he was staying. But she knew how to cherish the moment now.

She loved dancing with him. The way he looked into her eyes was enough. When he pressed his hand against her lower back, drawing her closer, she could feel how hard he was. She held him, determined to live in the moment for as long as it lasted.

He stopped moving and simply held her. It made her heart break and swell at the same time.

"Chloe." He didn't say her name; he growled it. She felt the vibration throughout her body. His lips were soft fire, burning, soothing, making her head spin. She fought against the desire pulsing within her. The heat, the need.

"I didn't think I'd see you again. I thought you moved on. Went back to your old life," she said.

"I'm here, *meu amor.*" There. She could see the tightness in his jaw, his shoulders. He was nervous again.

She swallowed the lump in her throat. "Why did you come back?"

Those dreamy eyes were full of emotion. "It has nothing at all to do with your father."

She blinked. "What?"

He shook his head. "That's another story. This is about us. I'm sorry I left and didn't call. But I didn't move on." He rubbed her arm, lifting chill bumps of delight across her skin. "I think you're stuck with me. You changed me, made me realize I want long-term. There's no going back. I want a meaningful life. I want real. More than anything in the world, I want you. You are the hole in my life that I couldn't fill." He pressed his forehead to hers. "Until I found you."

"Oh, Nicolas. You are what I've been missing, too. I was devastated when I thought I'd lost you."

"You can't lose me, because I love you, Chloe Harper." His grin slid sideways. "I've never said that to anyone before." As soft as a whisper, he said it again. "I love you." Pressing his lips to her temple, he whispered, "*Minha paixão*. Always. My Chloe. *Minha vida*."

She didn't recognize the Portuguese words, but they sounded like a prayer and felt like love. "I love you, too."

"I hurt you when I left. I'm sorry. I won't do it again. Give me a chance to make it up to you." The smoldering look he gave her sent a series of electric waves through her body.

"How do you plan on doing that?"

He grinned. "I do this thing with my mouth…"

# Epilogue

Nicolas leaned over and kissed her cheek. "You've got this. Just look at me when we sing and it will be easy."

They were sitting on a makeshift stage by the altar in the only church in Pueblicito. The place was completely packed and it felt like every person she'd ever known was staring at her, waiting for her to perform.

"Easy?" She squeaked. "What if I mess up my father's wedding?"

"That guy?" He pointed toward her dad, who was standing at the front of the church. "Look at him. He won't even hear us."

He was right. Dad had the biggest smile on his face as he rocked back and forth on his heels, waiting for Angel to come down the aisle. He couldn't stand still. Like a kid waiting to go to Disneyland. Matt and Jeff stood beside him in their matching tuxedos, patting him on the back and grinning like two fools. How could she be nervous at a time like this? Her family was together and happy. Even Mom. Claire, who was sitting right up front so she could get a good view, waved her kerchief. Chloe waved back.

They were all here because of her dad. Because Angel had convinced him to *seek redemption, make amends and forgive himself.*

In fact, RW's plans had worked for everyone. In the end he got his family back, and each one of them had found love.

Chloe let her gaze fall over her extended family. Julia's baby bump was showing now. Chloe couldn't wait to throw the baby shower. Henry was at the back of the church, excited to do his bit as the ring bearer. Michele actually sat next to Claire. The two of them seemed to have buried the hatchet, and Claire sang her praises about the best chef on the West Coast. Her mother seemed content now that she was welcomed back into the family. Her two brothers were happy in their jobs and lives. Everything was perfect except...

"Ready?" Nicolas asked her.

"No. Never. Not in a million years," Chloe said. She was never going to be comfortable singing in front of crowds. The recording studio, okay, but on a stage? No way.

"One and two and three..." Nicolas started strumming his guitar and she quickly joined him. His voice lifted over the crowd, richer and deeper than ever. She couldn't believe that he'd written a song for her, about her. Currently it was sitting at number three on the charts. She had no doubt it would hit number one. It was amazing. When he sang the haunting, emotional ballad about being lost at sea and going down for the last time, her chest squeezed. He was on his last breath, lost in darkness, when the pirate girl plucked him from the deep and taught him about light and love.

*My Pirate Girl.*

Chloe sang the chorus, which ended with, "I'm here. Just breathe. Just breathe."

They finished the song together, gazing into each other's eyes. The look he gave her made it hard to catch her own breath.

"I love you, Chloe."

"I love you, Nicolas." She leaned over and kissed him.

Applause erupted in the church. Chloe blinked, remembering where she was.

Lightness and love flowed through her. Her sacral chakra was wide-open, just like her heart. Nicolas had healed her, made her feel better about who she was and let her sing. He was a dream come true.

No, better. He was hers.

\* \* \* \* \*

# COMING NEXT MONTH FROM

## HARLEQUIN *Desire*

### Available July 1, 2019

---

**#2671 MARRIED IN NAME ONLY**

*Texas Cattleman's Club: Houston* • by Jules Bennett

Facing an explosive revelation about her real father, Paisley Morgan has no one to turn to except her ex, wealthy investigator Lucas Ford. Lucas has one condition for doing business with the woman who unceremoniously dumped him, though—a marriage of convenience to settle the score!

**#2672 RED HOT RANCHER**

by Maureen Child

Five years ago, Emma Williams left home for dreams of Hollywood—right before rancher Caden Hale could propose. Now she's back, older and wiser—and with a baby! Will the newly wealthy cowboy want a rematch?

**#2673 SEDUCED BY SECOND CHANCES**

*Dynasties: Secrets of the A-List* • by Reese Ryan

Singer-songwriter Jessica Humphrey is on the brink of fame when a performance brings her face-to-face with the one man she's always desired but could never have—her sister's ex, Gideon Johns. Will their unstoppable passion be her downfall? Or can she have it all?

**#2674 ONE NIGHT, WHITE LIES**

*The Bachelor Pact* • by Jessica Lemmon

When Reid Singleton buys the beautiful stranger a drink, he doesn't realize she's actually his best friend's little sister, Drew Fleming—until after he sleeps with her! Will their fledgling relationship survive...as even bigger family secrets threaten to derail everything?

**#2675 A CINDERELLA SEDUCTION**

*The Eden Empire* • by Karen Booth

Newly minted heiress Emma Stewart is desperate to be part of the powerful family she never knew. But when she realizes her very own Prince Charming comes from a rival family set on taking hers down, the stakes of seduction couldn't get higher...

**#2676 A TANGLED ENGAGEMENT**

*Takeover Tycoons* • by Tessa Radley

Hard-driving fashion executives Jay Black and Georgia Kinnear often butt heads. But Jay won't just stand by and let her controlling father marry her off to another man—especially when Jay has his own plan to make her his fake fiancée!

---

**YOU CAN FIND MORE INFORMATION ON UPCOMING HARLEQUIN® TITLES, FREE EXCERPTS AND MORE AT WWW.HARLEQUIN.COM.**

HDCNM0619

# Get 4 FREE REWARDS!

## We'll send you 2 FREE Books plus 2 FREE Mystery Gifts.

**Harlequin® Desire** books feature heroes who have it all: wealth, status, incredible good looks... everything but the right woman.

FREE Value Over $20

---

**YES!** Please send me 2 FREE Harlequin® Desire novels and my 2 FREE gifts (gifts are worth about $10 retail). After receiving them, if I don't wish to receive any more books, I can return the shipping statement marked "cancel." If I don't cancel, I will receive 6 brand-new novels every month and be billed just $4.55 per book in the U.S. or $5.24 per book in Canada. That's a savings of at least 13% off the cover price! It's quite a bargain! Shipping and handling is just 50¢ per book in the U.S. and 75¢ per book in Canada.* I understand that accepting the 2 free books and gifts places me under no obligation to buy anything. I can always return a shipment and cancel at any time. The free books and gifts are mine to keep no matter what I decide.

225/326 HDN GMYU

Name (please print)

Address                                                                          Apt. #

City                                      State/Province                    Zip/Postal Code

### Mail to the **Reader Service:**
**IN U.S.A.:** P.O. Box 1341, Buffalo, NY 14240-8531
**IN CANADA:** P.O. Box 603, Fort Erie, Ontario L2A 5X3

Want to try 2 free books from another series? Call 1-800-873-8635 or visit www.ReaderService.com.

---

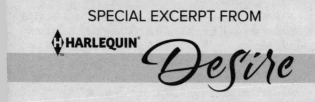
London-born Reid Singleton didn't know a damn thing about
women's shoes. So when he became transfixed by a pair on
the dance floor, fashion wasn't his dominating thought.

They were pink, but somehow also metallic, with long
Grecian-style straps crisscrossing delicate, gorgeous ankles.
He curled his scotch to his chest and backed into the shadows,
content to watch the woman who owned those ankles for a
bit.

From those pinkish metallic spikes, the picture only
improved. He followed the straps to perfectly rounded calves
and the outline of tantalizing thighs lost in a skirt that moved
when she did. The cream-colored skirt led to a sparkling
gold top. Her shoulders were slight, the swells of her breasts
snagging his attention for a beat, and her hair fell in curls over
those small shoulders. Dark hair with a touch of mahogany, or
maybe rich cherry. Not quite red, but with a notable amount
of warmth.

He sipped from his glass, again taking in the skirt, both flirty and fun in equal measures. A guy could get lost in there. Get lost in her.

An inviting thought, indeed.

The brunette spun around, her skirt swirling, her smile a seemingly permanent feature. She was lively and vivid, and even in her muted gold-and-cream ensemble, somehow the brightest color in the room. A man approached her, and Reid promptly lost his smile, a strange feeling of propriety rolling over him and causing him to bristle.

The suited man was average height with a receding hairline. He was on the skinny side, but the vision in gold simply smiled up at him, dazzling the man like she'd cast a spell. When she shook her head in dismissal and the man ducked his head and moved on, relief swamped Reid, but he still didn't approach her.

Careful was the only way to proceed, or so instinct told him. She was open but somehow skittish, in an outfit he couldn't take his eyes from. He hadn't been in a rush to approach the goddess like some of the other men in the room.

Reid had already decided to carefully choose his moment, but as she made eye contact, he realized he wasn't going to have to approach her.

She was coming to him.

One Night, White Lies
*by Jessica Lemmon,*
*available July 2019 wherever*
*Harlequin® Desire books and ebooks are sold.*

www.Harlequin.com

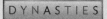

*Love Harlequin romance?*

## DISCOVER.

Be the first to find out about promotions, news and exclusive content!

 Facebook.com/HarlequinBooks

Twitter.com/HarlequinBooks

Instagram.com/HarlequinBooks

Pinterest.com/HarlequinBooks

ReaderService.com

## EXPLORE.

Sign up for the Harlequin e-newsletter and download a free book from any series at **TryHarlequin.com.**

## CONNECT.

Join our Harlequin community to share your thoughts and connect with other romance readers!
**Facebook.com/groups/HarlequinConnection**

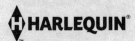

**ROMANCE WHEN
YOU NEED IT**

HSOCIAL2018

# THE WORLD IS BETTER WITH

*Romance*

0617

Harlequin has everything from contemporary, passionate and heartwarming to suspenseful and inspirational stories.

Whatever your mood,
we have a romance just for you!

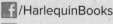